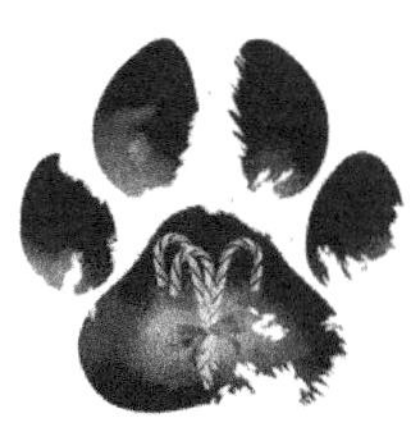

CANINES AND CANDY CANES

WHISKEY MYSTERY #3

In Your Face Ink LLC
9524 W. Camelback Road
#130-182
Glendale, AZ 85305
www.inyourfaceink.com
www.whiskeydogmysteries.com

First printed in the United States of America by In Your Face Ink LLC

ISBN: 978-1-7379733-7-9 (hardback)
ISBN: 978-1-7379733-8-6 (paperback)
ISBN: 978-1-7379733-9-3 (e-book)

Book design and cover by Rick Schank of Purple Couch Creative

For all humans who love and care for dogs and other animals.

COUNTDOWN TO CHRISTMAS

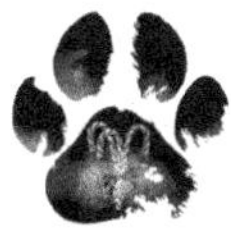

CHAPTER ONE

"**A**re you sure you can fit me in?" Sarah Carter, the twenty-eight-year-old proprietor of Carter's Canine Coiffure, asked Jared Greene, her friend, occasional date, the best barista in Cottageville, and graphic artist extraordinaire.

"Of course I can fit you in. I told you I'd meet you at the Coiffure on Sunday morning at ten." Jared didn't look at Sarah as he said those words. His focus was the library's big plate glass windows. Ever since he had gotten off work from Java and Juice at two p.m., he had been at the library. He hadn't been looking for books. He had been climbing up and down a ladder painting an outline of the holiday scene that Carole Binds, the head librarian, asked him to create "to bring some secular

Christmas joy" as she called it to one of the community's primary meeting places.

In fact, once word got out that Jared had sold his first graphic novel to a major New York publisher, the residents of Cottageville had started to look at him differently. No longer was he the six-foot-three auburn-haired coffee and croissant server at the most popular cafe in town. Suddenly he was an Artist, with a capital A, who just happened to enable their morning caffeine fixes.

And because of that shift in perspective, Jared was in demand to create holiday renderings on the windows of almost all of the businesses in town. So far he had painted children on sleds zipping down hills on the automatic doors of Cottageville Hospital's emergency room, oversized wrapped gifts and colorful candies on the every window of the elementary school, a hot cocoa and après ski scene on the windows at Java and Juice, cartoon children whose faces were awash with wonder at their gifts on the windows of the toy store, and a Dalmatian with a red bow around its neck at the firehouse. Jared had worked seven days a week for fourteen hours a day for the whole month of November—between his two jobs—and it was now December first, and Sarah wondered if he was sick of painting.

"If you are tired of this..." Sarah's voice trailed off.

Despite the near freezing temperature, Jared wore a buffalo check plaid flannel shirt over a thermal henley and jeans, as he couldn't paint big murals in a bulky coat and while wearing gloves. "Sarah," Jared said, finally looking at her.

She knew he was serious when he called her by name. Usually he joked and called her "mi'lady" in this whole silly chivalrous schtick they did. "Yes, Jared?" she asked, holding his green-eyed gaze.

"I *am* tired. Very tired. But this is also super inspiring for me. I came to Cottageville more than six years ago because I knew it would be a place that would give me the freedom and space to make art. And look at me now. I have my first book coming out with a major publisher next year. And our fine neighbors are finally recognizing me for my talent beyond frothed milk and foam art. I'm living my dreams and I'm loving every minute of it."

Sarah grinned at him. "I'm sure. I am so glad you are finally being seen for you and everything you contribute to this town and our lives and…well…to the world. It's exciting. I'm glad to be on this journey with you. But I am worried you are wearing yourself too thin. That's why I don't want you to feel obligated—"

He cut her off with a red paint speckled index finger to her lips. "Shhh. I'm glad you care about me and for my well-being. But seriously, painting a dog on the door of your shop will take me like fifteen minutes. Twenty tops. I'm gonna paint a portrait of Whiskey with a big candy cane in his mouth."

Whiskey, Sarah's almost seven-year-old Australian red heeler cattle dog, whined when he heard his name. He rubbed against Jared's left leg. Jared was one of his most favorite people in a sea of favorite people in their town.

Jared reached down and ruffled his ears. "You're such a good boy. Yes, you are," he said.

When Jared looked up at Sarah again, he said, "And when I'm done, you can pay me by taking me to brunch." He grinned.

"Perfect," Sarah said. "I'll make a reservation at Poached

Perfection for ten-thirty."

"Delightful." He kissed the end of her nose and then turned back to the library's windows. He picked up a container of green paint, pulled a brush from his back pocket, and climbed to the top of the ladder.

"Be careful up there," Sarah said to Jared, before addressing her dog. "Come on, Whiskey. Let's be on our way so Jared can work."

Like a grand marshal, Whiskey led the way up Main Street—though he stayed on the sidewalk—until they got to where the park began on the other side of the road. Whiskey set his butt on the snow-dusted pavement and waited until Cottageville's one street light turned green again, and it was safe for them to cross. Then, with his white-tipped tail in the air and a glance over his shoulder to make sure Sarah, wrapped in her navy blue winter jacket and multi-colored wool scarf, was following, he marched across the street and into the park's powdery snow topped grass where he promptly dropped to his side and rolled back and forth on his spine.

Laughter burst from Sarah at the canine version of a snow angel. "Does that feel good, boy?"

Whiskey wiggled his shoulders and butt forming c's and backwards c's before bouncing onto his four paws, shaking the dirt, grass, and snow from his coat, and resuming their walk. He followed the path that meandered through the park until he spied his friend Sascha, a German shepherd who lived with Cottageville Chief of Police James Order and his wife, Barbara. Chief James held a lime green ChuckIt! stick in one hand and flicked his wrist, which caused the orange and blue ball to go sailing. Like a greyhound after a rabbit, Sascha sprinted after the ball. And Whiskey took off after her.

Sarah jogged to keep up, but she felt more like the runt at the back of the pack. Sascha, with the ball in her mouth and Whiskey by her side, returned to Chief James before Sarah caught up to them. "Afternoon, Chief," she huffed.

"Sarah. Good to see you." He threw the ball again and the dogs took off. "Will you be at Winter Wonderland?"

Trish McGowan, Cottageville's mayor and Barbara Order's best friend since childhood, hosted a holiday event the first weekend in December every year. The festivities kicked off on Friday night when the mayor plugged in the hundreds of colorful lights wrapped around a majestic white pine, the tallest tree in Cottageville Park. And she gave a speech of gratitude and accolades to citizens who had done amazing things for the town over the past twelve months. That was followed by a scavenger hunt for the children. For the whole weekend, local businesses set up booths of games, arts and crafts, food and drinks, and merchandise for sale to help people get into the Christmas spirit. And people from all over descended on Cottageville like Swifties at one of Taylor's concerts. This one weekend was the town's peak tourism time.

For the past six seasons, Carter's Canine Coiffure had set up a table selling Christmas-, Hanukkah-, and Kwanzaa-themed bandannas, collars, and leashes, as well as donating gift certificates and services for the silent auction. All of the money raised was donated to the local food pantry that fed more than three hundred families each week.

Sarah said, "Whiskey and I wouldn't miss it. We are sharing a big booth with Java and Juice this year as I talked Ginger into selling her homemade dog biscuits as well as her fabulous food for humans."

Ginger Jones owned Java and Juice, and when Sarah had moved to Cottageville more than six years ago, she and Ginger struck up a friendship that quickly turned them into BFFs.

"Oh that's great. We should get some for Sascha's stocking. She can't get enough of those biscuits." Sascha had "only child status" in her household. Chief James used the lime green thrower to pick up the saliva-slick ball she dropped at his feet. "You tired yet?" he asked his dog. Her tongue protruded from the right side of her mouth and she was panting. But her body tensed, ready to go after the ball another time.

Whiskey looked from Sascha to Chief James and then lined up his shorter legs and body next to hers, imitating her stance. As soon as the ball snapped from the holder, they took off, pounding the ground in syncopated rhythm.

"They're so fast," Sarah said. She admired the way their muscles moved causing their fur to ripple. Whiskey may have been more barrel shaped than Sascha, but his breed had been created for herding cattle and keeping them in line, and that took speed. He stayed neck and neck with his longer legged friend.

This time, Sascha let Whiskey snatch the ball in his jaws. He smiled around it and raced back toward Chief James with Sascha running as his wing woman. Whiskey dropped the ball below the laces on Chief James' black leather boot, and it rolled from there to the ground. Then Whiskey collapsed on his belly with his arms bent at the elbows like he was doing a sphinx pose in yoga class.

Looking down at him, Chief James chuckled. "I think we're done. Barbara is expecting us home for supper anyway. Come on, Sascha.

Nice seeing you, Sarah."

Whiskey stood and sniffed his friend's ear as a good-bye. Sascha stood stock-still and let him.

Chief James scratched Whiskey's forehead. "Thank you for playing with us, Whiskey."

"Thank you for permitting him to," Sarah said. "Let's go, boy." She motioned for Whiskey to walk the path with her. He stayed by her side as Sarah contemplated the contents of her fridge and what she could make for her supper.

They had gone twenty steps when a screech of tires cut through Sarah's thoughts. A loud BOOM followed and then half a second later, the shattering of glass pierced the chilled air. The three sounds happened so fast in succession that Sarah froze in shock.

"What the heck?" she said aloud. She turned and looked toward the park entrance where she saw Chief James running like he was trying to break a land speed record. Sascha sprinted beside him with ease.

In a split second decision, Sarah ran after them, toward the sound of the accident. Whiskey passed her when they were halfway across the park. His mouth was open and his tongue hung low. "Slow down, Whisk," Sarah panted.

Whiskey slammed on his brakes at the entrance, thumped his tail against the ground, and waited for her to catch up.

Lots of people—in various manners of dress—were now pouring onto Main Street. Some women wore aprons over their clothes, like they had been in the middle of cooking dinner. Jackets and appropriate winter attire were being pulled on and zipped as people raced from their residences and shops. None of them paid attention to Whiskey or Sarah. Their eyes were searching two blocks down Main Street, where the trailer end of a semi-truck could be seen at an almost jackknifed angle to the street, blocking traffic on both the north and southbound sides.

The truck's cab was crumpled. It had crashed through the big plate glass windows of Cottageville's pride and joy, its library.

Sarah couldn't see the ladder Jared had been standing on. And she couldn't see Jared.

Her heart slammed in her chest causing her to gasp.

"Jared!" Sarah screamed, before she ran faster than she ever had in her life, weaving between her neighbors and strangers, with Whiskey close on her heels.

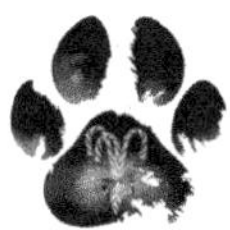

CHAPTER TWO

The chaotic scene outside Cottageville's library was a stark contrast to the peaceful and enjoyable time Sarah had been experiencing just moments ago in the park. People hurried toward the scene of the accident, their voices filled with urgency and concern. One woman was standing as still as an oak tree trunk and crying.

Sarah's heart raced as she pushed through the crowd, Whiskey weaving skillfully by her side. She scanned what she could see of the wreckage of the semi-truck, part of its cab twisted, embedded into the library's facade.

"Jared!" Sarah called out again, her voice trembling with fear.

She pushed closer, ignoring the cold wind biting at her cheeks. She could see Chief James and Sascha already at the scene, assessing the situation. She heard the siren's wail from the ambulance and the "eee ooo eee ooo" of a fire truck approaching the scene.

"Everyone get back," Chief James bellowed. "Let the first responders through."

The crowd on Main Street parted faster than the Red Sea for Moses before the ladder truck and the aid car screeched to a stop. More sirens could be heard in the distance.

Sarah's eyes darted around, searching desperately for any sign of her friend. Whiskey moved closer, like he wanted to help Sarah. His nose was to the ground, following the scent of something. Then he stopped and sniffed the air.

Shattered glass and debris littered the ground.

"Be careful, boy," Sarah said, worried he'd cut his paw on a shard.

But Whiskey trotted forward with renewed determination. Sarah followed him until she spotted Carole Binds standing inside at a safe distance from where the library wall of windows had been. Tears streamed down her face as she clutched a stack of books to her chest.

"Carole," Sarah called out, hoping for answers.

Carole made eye contact, and her expression was a cocktail of equal parts shock and sorrow.

"Oh, Sarah," Carole gasped. "Jared…He was up there…painting… and then…"

Sarah's heart plummeted to her feet. Her eyes again scanned the wreckage for movement. She now noticed part of the aluminum ladder curved around the mangled front end of the truck's grill.

Was Jared under the truck? Sarah knelt on the ground and looked, but she saw no one and nothing but broken glass and bits of metal and a puddle of some kind. *Was it leaking gasoline?* Sarah wondered if Chief James had seen it.

Movement on the truck caught Sarah's eye. Volunteer medic Walter Parks climbed onto the first stair of the cab and pulled open the door. Sarah could see that the driver was in the cab, unmoving, and collapsed face down over the steering wheel. Sarah spied a bloody gash on his forehead.

She watched Walter put two fingers on the guy's wrist to check for his pulse as Wendy Parks, the town's other main medic and Walter's wife, climbed into the cab from the passenger side.

Sarah was rooted to the bit of sidewalk on which she stood, feeling like she was watching a film and not real life. She saw Walter shake his head at Wendy, and then they both climbed down from the truck.

Walter walked a few feet to Chief James and said something that Sarah couldn't hear.

Chief James pulled out his phone from his jeans pocket and made a call.

The only word Sarah heard as her eyes roamed the wreckage was "coroner." Tears sprung to her green eyes and trickled down her cheeks. She wiped them away with her hands.

The fire personnel were working diligently, moving overturned shelving and books, lifting large pieces of glass and bent and broken pieces of steel. Sarah could tell they were checking on the stability of the building and searching for anyone trapped in the debris. They frequently told people to get back, as did Chief James, once he ended his phone call.

Officer Beams and Officer Grimes pushed their way through the crowd and set up saw horses and police tape to create a perimeter around the truck. Sarah had been forced back behind the perimeter, and Whiskey had returned to her side. He pressed against her leg, and his presence became a comforting weight.

She wondered where on earth Jared could be. *He couldn't have just disappeared. He may have been thrown though, if the truck hit when he was atop the ladder.* Sarah scanned the area across the crowd and the road. She hoped to get a glimpse of his red hair somewhere.

Suddenly, Sarah spied Walter and Wendy carrying a stretcher toward the library building. Their focused movement was a dichotomy to the chaos of search and recovery around them. And that gave Sarah hope. She took a deep breath and tried to steady her nerves and see where they were going. Sarah strained her neck as they walked through what used to be the wall of windows. She stood on her tiptoes, trying to get a better look.

An arm slipped around Sarah and she was squeezed to someone's side, which made her heart skip a beat until she inhaled the scent of cinnamon, yeast, and sugar. Sarah relaxed. It was the signature scent of Ginger Jones, her BFF and Jared's employer at Java and Juice. Ginger's usually cheerful face was now pale with worry and she seemed slightly out of breath. Her blond hair was covered by a red knit cap that matched the mittens that peeked from her cream colored down jacket.

"Sarah, I heard...Is Jared okay?" Her voice was barely above a whisper.

Sarah shook her head, unable to find the words.

Ginger wrapped her arms around Sarah, offering silent support. They stood together, watching and waiting as the rescue efforts continued. Minutes felt like hours as Sarah's thoughts tumbled like puppies play-fighting, each thought jockeying to be dominant. She replayed her conversation with Jared in her mind, the easy banter and the plans for brunch now overshadowed by fear and uncertainty. *Would she ever talk to him again?*

She strained her neck higher but couldn't see Walter or Wendy or the stretcher.

As if reading her mind, Ginger said, "They'll find him. I know they will. And he'll be okay."

"How can you be so sure?" Sarah hiccupped on a sob. "Did you see the ladder?"

"No..." Ginger's voice trailed off.

"It's embedded on the front of the truck. Or at least part of it is. I think the feet of it are slightly under the truck. That doesn't bode well for anyone on top of it."

Ginger hugged Sarah again. "I agree, love. But he isn't on or under the truck, otherwise they would have found him by now. Maybe he wasn't on the ladder at the time. He could have been taking a break or climbed down for more paint or even gone inside the library to pee."

"Or maybe he was thrown—" Sarah's comment was interrupted as a murmur and a cheer went through the crowd. Her heart leaped into her throat as she saw movement at the edge of the wreckage and realized that's where the Parks were. Firefighters were carefully lifting shelving and glass, holding it from the ground, while Walter

Parks carefully pulled Jared out from under the debris. His clothing was covered in dust and paint splatters of white, blue, green, red, and yellow.

When his head turned toward the crowd, Sarah realized she had been holding her breath. An audible whoosh left her body. "He's alive," she said to no one in particular.

"He is indeed," Ginger said.

Jared's head moved, scanning the crowd, as Walter helped him sit on the stretcher. When Jared's eyes caught Sarah's, he gave her a weak smile. And Sarah burst into a fresh round of tears, but of joy this time, not of frustration and sorrow.

Walter and Wendy told Jared to lie back and then strapped him down. They raised the bed and started to guide it to their ambulance. Sarah, Whiskey, and Ginger cut through the crowd to meet them at the ambulance's rear doors.

Walter and Wendy opened the doors as Jared murmured, his voice hoarse. "Guess I made quite the mess, huh?"

Sarah gently clasped one of his hands in hers, while Ginger held his other. Sarah smiled at Jared as her eyes overflowed with tears. She brushed some dust from his stubbled cheek. "You scared me half to death," she admitted.

"Sorry about that." Jared winced as he moved on the gurney.

"What hurts?" Ginger asked.

"My ankle. My back. My pride." Jared grinned at his own joke.

Whiskey stood on his hind legs and tried to reach Jared with his front paws.

"Hey, bud," Jared said. He let go of Sarah's hand and reached for

Whiskey's paw. "I'm gonna be okay. Really I am."

"You will, but hold still," Walter said, letting Jared know they were pushing him into the ambulance.

"Down, Whiskey," Sarah said, grabbing a hold of his collar. "The Parks need to get Jared to the hospital. Jared, Ginger and I will meet you there."

Sarah glanced at Ginger for confirmation, and her BFF nodded her knit cap covered head.

Walter shut Wendy in the back of the ambulance with Jared, and he went around to the driver's side and started the engine. He tapped the horn lightly letting those assembled around his ride know that he was moving out. And because the semi-truck's trailer was blocking Main Street, which was the direct route to the hospital seven blocks away, Walter turned right and then right again, taking an alternate way to the ER.

Sarah turned and searched the still-assembled crowd to see if there was an easy path up Main Street. But the coroner had just shown up and the block was still a congested mess of lookie-loos. So she and Ginger followed the path of the Parks' ambulance, with Whiskey keeping pace alongside them.

"Hey, wait," Sarah said. "What am I thinking? I can't take Whiskey to the ER."

"That's true," Ginger said. "I didn't think of that either."

"Hang on a sec." Sarah pulled her phone from the back pocket of her jeans, which was buried under her coat. She flipped through her contacts and then pushed a number. "Hello, Gladys. May I drop Whiskey off at your house to visit with your girls? Yes, I've been on

Main Street. Jared was taken to the ER, and Ginger and I want to go check on him, but Whiskey can't come."

Sarah listened for thirty seconds before she said, "Yes, thank you. Thank you very much." And then she disconnected and looked at Ginger. "Gladys said she and Janice are making supper and that Whiskey is welcome to join."

Janice Jenkins was Sarah's next door neighbor and Gladys' best friend. They were both close to eighty years old but seemed young for their ages as they went to yoga classes at the Presbyterian Church and walked Gladys' two mini poodles, Kahlo and Cassatt, around Cottageville. Gladys was a retired high school art teacher, and Janice spent her career working for the U.S. government's alphabet agencies, and now did some private security consulting when called upon by governments and museums around the world.

Gladys was not only Sarah's friend, but the closest thing she had to a grandmother, since hers had passed more than six years before, leaving her cherished memories and the house in Cottageville. Gigi, her grandmother, had been one of Gladys' closest friends so Sarah had known Gladys since her childhood when she flew from Seattle to Iowa and spent part of each summer with Gigi.

Ten minutes later, Sarah and Ginger said good-bye to Whiskey at Gladys' front door. He barely acknowledged them as he romped into the living room to play with his small, curly haired friends who jumped all over him in their joy. Gladys gave Sarah a quick hug and told her to be safe and that she'd keep Whiskey as long as necessary. "You go make sure Jared is okay, dear." Gladys patted the arm of Sarah's coat and gazed into her eyes with kindness.

Sarah was filled with gratitude. She grabbed ahold of Ginger's arm, said, "Good-bye" to Gladys and Janice, and speed-walked the last few blocks to the hospital.

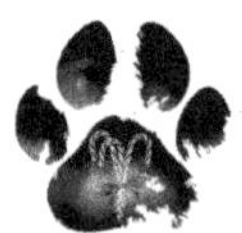

CHAPTER THREE

As they approached the emergency room, Sarah was struck by the vivid primary colors in the scene of children sledding that Jared had painted on the doors. The children seemed so full of life with rosy cheeks and smiles, accompanied by a barking dachshund chasing down a snow-covered hill after a blue snow-suit wearing boy on a lime green snow saucer. She was sure as he had painted that he had no idea he'd be brought by ambulance through those very same doors.

Sarah shook her head to clear the mental image.

Ginger seemed like she read Sarah's mind when she said, "He does gorgeous work. And I'm sure he's fine. I mean, he even joked with us before the Parks drove him away."

They checked in at the desk, where Ginger introduced Sarah as Jared's girlfriend. It was a bit of a stretch since they had never defined themselves. But as they walked toward orange and metal plastic chairs in the waiting room, Ginger said, "I thought it was the only way they'd let us back there."

"It's okay," Sarah said. She removed her jacket before sitting on a chair and her eyes wandered around the room. The place was half filled and the tension was as dense as a husky's fur. Sarah sighed.

"How are things with Daniel and the remodel?" Ginger had been dating Daniel Snyder, owner of Buck and Son Hardware, for more than eight months, first secretly as they didn't want the whole town talking about them before they figured out if they wanted to be a couple. They had known each other for forever, as both were from Cottageville, and Ginger had gone to school with Daniel and his high school sweetheart who later became his wife. She had died during pregnancy, and Daniel spent years mourning the loss of her and his unborn child, before asking Ginger on a date.

Now, most people in Cottageville knew they were romantically involved, since in October, Daniel had sold the house he and his wife had owned, and he and Ginger bought an old two-story farmhouse together on the town outskirts. Last month, Daniel had torn apart the kitchen to do a full rebuild with a six-burner range and double ovens and commercial size stainless steel fridge and freezer so Ginger could just as easily bake at home as she did in her cafe. Sarah had gone with Ginger to look at cabinet options and was thrilled when Ginger settled on a slate blue color as it really popped against the white trim of the big kitchen windows and the white marble she had chosen for the counters.

"He's so loving and thoughtful. Did I tell you he made me a big, walnut heart-shaped cutting board as a surprise?" Ginger grinned and her blue eyes sparkled.

"No, you didn't mention that. That's so sweet."

"The remodel itself is going slowly, but that's what I expected since we are doing most of it ourselves. And we are both super busy with our businesses and with Christmas stuff. I figure we'll be done before next summer," Ginger joked.

"Or at least by Easter," Sarah said.

"Something like that." Ginger squirmed in her chair like she was uncomfortable. "I wonder how long we'll have to wait." She stood and walked toward the desk, just as someone opened the double doors. A woman in a wheelchair was pushed by a scrubs wearing attendant through the waiting area. They stopped between the big glass sliding doors, and the attendant helped the woman into her coat before pushing her outside and helping her from the wheelchair into the back seat of a waiting taxi. And then the attendant brought the empty wheelchair back into the hospital as the taxi pulled away.

Sarah and Ginger watched it all in silence. Sarah didn't recognize the woman but felt sad she had no one to pick her up. She opened her mouth to say something about that to Ginger, but her BFF was walking toward the desk and Sarah heard Ginger ask where the restroom was located.

Sarah pulled her phone from her purse and checked for missed messages. She wondered if Jared had his phone on him and if it had survived the crash. She texted, "Hey, my lord, what's going on back there? Are you okay?"

She watched as her message reported "Delivered" and wished it to change to "Read," but minutes passed with nothing. Or at least it felt like minutes to Sarah.

But what she really wanted wasn't just "Read". Her heart longed for those three dots that signified someone was typing.

Sarah checked her email and watched some funny dog videos without sound so she didn't disturb those around her while she waited to hear from Jared. Five to ten minutes later—she lost track of time—Sarah wondered what the heck was keeping Ginger so long.

Suddenly she saw Ginger's red cap come around the corner before the rest of her BFF. Ginger's head was down. She was concentrating on not spilling coffee from two lidless paper cups.

She handed one to Sarah. "I found a coffee machine down the hall. And here—." She reached into her jacket pocket and pulled out a cellophane wrapped package of powdered sugar donuts. "It was the best I could do."

After she sat, Ginger pulled out a second package of donuts, chocolate with chocolate icing, and said, "I'll give you half of this pack if you give me half of yours."

Sarah, who was mid sip of the black acrid liquid, said, "Deal." She set her cup on a nearby table and ripped open the package of donuts and handed three powdered ones to Ginger.

"I thought the sugar in these might make this swill more palatable."

"Certainly not the level I'm used to, but caffeine and sugar always work in a pinch." Sarah accepted three dark chocolate sticky rounds from Ginger. "Thank you very much." She bit into a chocolate donut first and then dipped the remainder of the donut in the coffee.

"Any word yet?" Ginger asked, before taking a bite of powdered sugar donut causing the white powder to poof into the air like a miniature snow squall in front of her.

"Nope. I texted like fifteen minutes ago, but Jared didn't answer." Sarah opened the messaging app. "He hasn't even read it, actually."

"Are we sure he even has his phone?"

"No idea," Sarah said, taking another bite of donut.

Gingered eyed the registration counter with interest, so Sarah turned her head in that direction. "Do you know her?" Sarah asked, referring to a rosy-cheeked Rubenesque woman in her thirties who now sat in the chair at the registration desk. The woman who had been manning the desk pulled her purse from somewhere below and bid the new woman a good night.

"Yes. Rebecca Majors. Regular at Java and Juice. Always gets an apple cinnamon muffin or an eclair and a twenty-ounce mocha with whip. I'll be right back." Ginger handed Sarah her half full cup of coffee and shoved the remaining donuts into her coat pocket. And then she approached the registration desk.

"Hi, Rebecca. It's Ginger from Java and Juice. My employee Jared is back there."

Sarah couldn't hear what Rebecca said, but she saw the woman's mauve lips move.

"Yes, I know. The whole thing is a tragedy. Anyway, I was wondering if there was a way for you to check to see how he's doing. His girlfriend is with me and she'd really like to go back and see him."

Rebecca's lips moved again, but again Sarah couldn't hear what she said. Then Rebecca's fingers flew over the computer keyboard in a flurry of activity and she stared at the screen with her lips pursed. Her eyes made contact with Ginger, before Rebecca picked up the phone and spoke into the receiver.

When she hung up, she said something to Ginger again, and Ginger said, "Thank you," and returned to where Sarah was seated. Sarah handed her the cup of coffee as Ginger said, "She checked on him and they are almost ready for us to come back. He broke a bone in his leg so they are setting a cast. Then we can see him."

"Is that the only thing he broke?"

"As far as I know. She said they did x-rays and some scans. We'll know more in a bit." Ginger sat back down next to Sarah. She took a sip of her coffee and pulled the donuts out of her coat pocket and ate one and then another without saying anything. After another swig of coffee, Ginger turned toward Sarah and softly asked, "Has today put anything into perspective for you?"

Sarah looked into her BFF's eyes. "Are you asking if I love him or want more from our relationship?"

"Yes. I mean, we could have lost him today." Ginger almost whispered the last part.

"Yes, we could have. And I felt the pain of that. Jared is someone I love. Very much. I think he loves me, too. But is he 'the one'? I'm not sure." Sarah finished her final powdered sugar donut and emptied her coffee cup in one go.

"I'm not sure 'the one' is a real thing," Ginger said. "I mean, I don't think we get just one other person. I think we love many different people in many different ways. I'm glad Daniel doesn't think he only gets 'one'."

Sarah's voice sounded strained when she said, "I didn't mean it like that. You, Daniel, his wife. That's different."

"It's all still love," Ginger said. "Someone once told me that 'love is an extremely high tolerance for another person's faults.' It is, in a way, because it's that tolerance that helps us live with other people. You and Jared have so much fun together and seem to light each other up. I think you would have missed that if things had turned out differently today."

Sarah's eyes filled with tears. "Yes," she admitted, "I would have felt a giant sucking hole in my life and in my heart."

The corners of Ginger's mouth quivered as if she was trying not to laugh at the description. She reached for Sarah's hand. "Yes, Sarah. That's what I thought. So maybe you two should both overcome your fears and date properly and see where this thing goes."

Sarah shrugged. "Maybe. If he is still able to go, I offered to take him to brunch on Sunday. Maybe that would be a good time to discuss it."

"And if he can't go to brunch, maybe you could bring brunch to him. Just a thought."

Sarah smiled and squeezed Ginger's hand. "When did you get so wise?"

Ginger laughed. "Maybe since I'm in love, I want to see the people I care about find love, too." As soon as the words were out of her mouth, the ER's outer glass doors opened and Daniel Snyder rushed in, his eyes scanning the waiting room until they landed on Ginger. He took long strides toward them. "How are you doing? How is Jared? Is he going to be okay?" Words rolled from his mouth like tumbleweeds across the desert.

Ginger patted the empty chair next to her. When he was within reach, she kissed his lips quickly and then said, "We are well though as Shakespeare said, 'waiting is hell'. We were told that Sarah will be permitted to see Jared shortly, after they set and cast his leg, or something like that."

"So, he broke his leg. Anything else?" Daniel asked, his brown eyes wide.

"Nothing was mentioned, but we don't know for sure."

A nurse in royal blue scrubs burst through the double ER doors. "Sarah Carter, can you come here please?"

Sarah stood and looked from Ginger to Daniel. "I'll text you some answers," she promised as she walked to the doors.

"Follow me," the nurse said. "He's asked for you a few times."

"Is he okay?" Sarah asked.

"He will be," the nurse insisted. "It could have been so much worse." She shook her head as if to dislodge the possibilities from her brain.

Sarah followed the nurse down the hallway and through a maze of curtained spaces. She noticed most of the beds were filled with people and one or two of them were moaning. That hurt her heart.

But when they stood at the last curtained space and she stepped through the industrial strength gray drapes, she grinned as big as the Cheshire cat mirroring the look on Jared's face.

CHAPTER FOUR

"Mi'lady," Jared said. "Sorry for the fright." He stiffly held out his arm and motioned like he meant to bow, but he winced when his head and spine did a small dip.

She rushed toward him and wanted to throw her arms around him but stopped short. She wasn't sure where he was hurt and didn't want to make him feel pain. "Hi. How are you?" She stood by his bed.

His right leg and foot to his knee were in a plaster cast atop the sheets, and the hospital gown hit high on his thigh. He had a small cut into his left eyebrow that Sarah hadn't noticed when Jared was being whisked away on the stretcher by the Parks. And underneath his eyes looked darker now, with either bruising or shadow. He had scratches and cuts on his arms. It looked like the nurses had scrubbed most of the paint away from his skin to reveal the minor abrasions like he had been struck by hundreds of shards of glass.

"I feel like I was hit by a truck." Jared laughed at his own joke before wincing and steadying his left ribs with his right hand.

"Because you were. Or the ladder was. Where were you when the truck smashed into the library?" She covered his hand with hers, as she gazed into his eyes.

"I was atop the ladder—you know on that top step they tell you not to stand on—which the docs tell me was a good thing, as the force threw me as opposed to the truck trapping and crushing me."

Sarah grimaced and admitted, "I saw the ladder. It looked almost embedded into the truck's grill."

"Better it than me." Jared gave her a lopsided grin.

"I'm glad you have retained your sense of humor."

"It could be the pain pills," Jared joked.

"Anything broken besides your leg?"

"Miraculously no. Ribs are bruised as is much of the rest of me, along with my ego." Jared grinned again. "Doc said I may feel worse tomorrow. They are keeping me overnight for observations. My head doesn't look concussed, but they want to be sure."

"I can pick you up tomorrow and take you home, or even take you to my house if you don't want to be alone. Whiskey is a great healer." Sarah smiled at her own joke.

"A heeler who heals. They all should." He returned her smile. "I'd appreciate it very much, Sarah, if you could get me when I'm released.

And if you are okay if people talk, may I stay with you for the first day or two? Also, can you let Ginger know I'm not going to make it to work tomorrow?"

"Um, yeah. I think she's already figured that out," Sarah said. "She's in the waiting room with Daniel. Oh, and that's right, I promised to text her an update." Sarah pulled her phone from her back pocket.

"Feel free," Jared said, using his free hand to cover a yawn. He leaned his head back against the pillow and closed his eyes.

Sarah texted a quick message to Ginger before she said, "I should let you rest." She leaned toward him and lightly brushed her lips against his cheek.

He opened his eyes.

"I'm so glad you're okay. Can you text me when you are being discharged?"

"Um, I don't have my phone. I'm not sure where it is or even if it is still functioning."

"I'll text John Beams and ask him to keep his eyes open for an iPhone in the debris."

"Thank you. And Sarah, I'm so glad you came to the ER. You're the best." He stifled a yawn before saying, "Excuse me."

"No need. You've been through so much. Get some sleep—or at least as much as you can in the hospital—and I'll see you in the morning, if they let me. Oh, and just so you know, Ginger told them we are a couple." Sarah whispered the last part.

Jared tilted his head. "Sounds good to me." He grinned showing his teeth, and this reminded Sarah of the way Whiskey smiled.

"We'll talk once they are sure you don't have a head injury," Sarah teased. She squeezed one of his hands. "Good night, Jared. Whiskey sends his love."

"He's a good boy."

"He is. I'll see you tomorrow." Sarah walked back through the floor length curtain and down the hall and followed the signs to the exit. Ginger and Daniel stood when they saw Sarah come through the white Emergency Room double doors.

"How's he look?" Ginger asked.

"His leg is in a cast. His spirit is still high and joking, though high could be because of meds," Sarah quipped. "He wanted me to apologize that he will not be at work in the morning."

"Daniel and I were just discussing that I'm going to need at least part-time help, not only because of this but through the holiday season. Know anyone?"

"Not off the top of my head, but I'll ask around." Sarah grabbed her jacket from the chair near Ginger and put it on. "Come on. I want to get Whiskey and go home. I know you have an early day tomorrow and so do I. They are keeping Jared for the night for observations, but he asked me to pick him up when he's discharged. I've offered for him to stay with me until he's in better shape."

"Ooo-la-la," Ginger said, wiggling her eyebrows.

Sarah frowned at her friend. "He's gonna need some help."

Daniel said, 'That's very nice of you, Sarah. Plus, the love of a dog helps everything."

"Exactly. And Whiskey considers Jared his best bud."

"It's because of all of those treats, you know." Ginger grinned knowingly as they exited the hospital. "How about if Daniel gives you a lift to Gladys'?"

"Thank you." They walked toward Daniel's extended cab pickup. Sarah climbed up into the back seat. "I appreciate both of you coming here with me."

"Of course," Ginger said. "Jared means a lot to us, too."

"I can't believe all he has is a broken leg." Daniel started the engine and turned on the heater to full blast.

"He's got cuts and bruises and probably bruises he doesn't even know he has yet. But yes, it's a miracle that's all."

Within minutes, they pulled up in front of Gladys' one-story house. Sarah said her goodbyes to Ginger and Daniel. Before she reached the front door, Sarah heard the barks of Whiskey, Cassatt, and Kahlo from inside the house and Gladys saying, "Just a minute, Whiskey. Let me get the door open."

Sarah chuckled to herself.

"Come on in, dear." Wearing a pastel lilac tracksuit over a white t-shirt, Gladys stood aside and asked, "Would you like a cup of tea?"

"Yes, but no, I really need to get home. I so appreciate you caring for Whiskey at the spur of the moment. I saw Jared and he's doing really well, all things considered. He broke his leg and he has some abrasions, but he should make a full recovery. They are keeping him tonight, but he will be released tomorrow."

"That's good news," Gladys said, clutching Sarah's hand with one of her bent, arthritic ones. "Especially since we heard the driver died at the scene."

"Yes," Sarah said. "It's sad, but I'm glad Jared will be okay." Sarah kissed Gladys' cheek and said goodbye to Kahlo and Cassatt. "Come on, Whiskey. Let's go home."

They walked down Main Street and cut across the park, which was mostly empty. *How quickly things change,* Sarah thought. They had been heading home through the park hours ago and now, Jared was injured and would move in with them while he recovered. *I guess that will give us time to figure out what we are to one another.*

The next morning on the way to work, Sarah and Whiskey stopped by Java and Juice to find the line almost to the door. Ginger was behind the counter by herself, taking orders, frothing milk, brewing coffee, and plating pastries, like an octopus grabbing things here and there.

Whiskey, who often approached the counter as soon as he entered the cafe, stayed right by Sarah's side in the line, like he sensed now was not the time to add to Ginger's stress. "Good boy," Sarah said, scratching the white fur on the space between his brown ears.

Ten minutes later, when Sarah made it to the front of the line, Ginger said, "Morning." She took Sarah's empty to-go tumbler and automatically filled it with black coffee and handed it back. "What will you have? I recommend the gingered salmon salads for your lunch, and I tried a new recipe last night when I couldn't sleep and came in early: candy cane scones with dark chocolate chunks."

"Oh, yum! Yes, please. Two of each."

Ginger added them to the bag and told Sarah the total. She touched her card to the terminal and added a forty percent tip as a way to bless her bestie who was flying solo. "Next," Ginger said, greeting the person behind Sarah whom Sarah had never seen before, a man wearing faded jeans, work boots, and a blue ski jacket with a dark brown oiled leather cowboy hat.

Before she stepped aside, Sarah said to Ginger, "I'll find you someone. I promise."

"Thanks," Ginger said to Sarah before, "What can I get you?" to the man.

When Sarah and Whiskey exited the cafe, fought the wind to walk one block south, and were about to turn onto the street that housed Carter's Canine Coiffure, she noticed a white van sporting an outlined caricature of a dog in a half wine barrel bathtub parked at the curb. "Moe's Mobile Grooming" and a phone number was on each side of the van and across the back doors and on the hood.

"Hmm," Sarah said to Whiskey. "I've never seen that van before." The area code of Moe's number wasn't the same as Cottageville and the surrounding county. She wondered if Moe was just passing through.

When Sarah got to the Coiffure she found her business already unlocked and her assistant, twenty-year-old Emily Colt, wearing long leather gloves for protection while trimming the nails of Chutney the chihuahua, who was baring his teeth and snapping toward her.

"Hi, Em."

"Hey, Sarah. This little Tasmanian devil is acting out even more than usual. He's been here ten minutes and I've only done one paw. George brought him in and said he'd be back soon. He had to sign for a delivery at the store." George owned Produce and More, Cottageville's only grocery store, and it literally had produce, meats, household goods, and a whole lot more, in the same way Buck and Son sold more than just hardware.

Whiskey raced under the counter as if he wanted to help Emily calm the scared little dog. He stood up on his hind legs with his front feet trying to stretch to the counter top, but Chutney snapped in Whiskey's direction so the red heeler returned all four of his feet to the floor. His brows furrowed like he was worried as his milk chocolate brown eyes pleaded with Chutney.

"Thanks for trying to help," Emily said to Whiskey. Her hair was dyed black with hot pink at the tips of the spikes that stood out all over her head. She wore black Doc Marten lace up boots on her feet and a black long sleeve sweater dress, with one of the Coiffure's denim aprons with multi-colored dog prints on it over the top of her dress. The leather gloves, which Sarah had bought specifically for when they had to deal with Chutney, covered the sleeves of Emily's dress all the way to her elbows.

"I'll help you as soon as I put the salads in the fridge," Sarah said, taking them into the back room and grabbing her apron off a hook. "We have Christmasy scones as a reward when we are done with the devil."

"Oooh, yum," Emily said. "Hey, I heard about the accident and Jared and everything. He's going to be alright, right? And what's Ginger doing without him? She must have been slammed this morning."

"She is. And she asked if I knew of anyone looking for a part-time job. She needed extra help for the holidays anyway, and then when this happened…" Sarah's voice trailed off as she shivered remembering the sounds of what she thought were an explosion. She never wanted to hear that again as long as she lived. She put her hands on Chutney's shoulders, holding him still and keeping her fingers out of biting range.

Emily picked up his right front paw and got to work. It went so much smoother with two of them holding onto the four-pound terror. "Taylor's been looking for a job," Emily said. Taylor had black hair and pale skin not unlike Johnny Depp in *Edward Scissorhands*. He lived with an iguana named Iggy, and Taylor had a huge crush on Emily.

"Can you text him to go see Ginger today?"

"Sure, as soon as we are done here."

"Thanks. I'll let Ginger know and maybe she can hire him on the spot."

"That would be amazing," Emily said, just as George walked through the front door of the Coiffure. Whiskey ran to greet him and wagged his tail as George patted his head.

"Hey, Sarah. Whiskey. Chuts not done yet?"

"He wasn't very nice to Emily so she couldn't get very far, but she'll be done in thirty seconds." Emily was clipping the last three nails on the dog's back left paw. That was all she had left.

Though the cost of the nail clipping was ten dollars, George threw a twenty on the counter. "I know what a pain she can be, which is why we don't do it ourselves," he said, scooping Chutney from the counter and carrying the dog under his arm as if she were a football. "I appreciate the good job you both do. Keep the change. Thank you."

With that, he left the Coiffure.

CHAPTER FIVE

Emily removed the big leather gloves as Sarah pulled the scones out of the Java and Juice bag and placed them on paper towels. "These look so good," Emily said, eying the chunks of chocolate that protruded from the dough.

Sarah picked up hers and took a bite. The peppermint hit her sinuses before the bittersweetness of the dark chocolate, the sugar in the scone itself, and the candy pieces. She chewed thoughtfully and swallowed, then said, "Ginger has a hit on her hands. I hope she's making these for the festival."

"She must," Emily said, closing her eyes as she chewed. When she swallowed, she opened her eyes, picked up her phone, and texted

Taylor. Sarah texted Ginger saying she found her part-time help.

After Sarah swallowed a few more bites of her scone and washed it down with coffee she asked, "Have you seen the Moe's Mobile Grooming van around town?"

"Last weekend I saw it parked on Main Street. You know that vacant storefront where there is the holiday pop-up candy shop? It was parked in front of there."

"Did you see the driver of it?"

Emily shook her head and her hair didn't move. "Nope. Have you been in that candy pop-up yet?"

"No. Have you?" Sarah finished the rest of her scone and coffee, just as the front door of the Coiffure opened and her friend Officer Candace Grimes walked in wearing civilian clothing of jeans, evergreen wellies, and a navy blue puffy jacket with a blue and tan plaid scarf tucked into the neck. She carried her mini lop rabbit named Maple in her arms. Whiskey ran to greet them.

After Candace had rescued the bunny in August, she had given it time to settle in before inviting Sarah and Whiskey over for an evening. At first Maple didn't know what to make of the curious dog or if he was a threat, but Whiskey laid down on the carpet and put his chin on his front paws and stayed still. Eventually, the rabbit came to him, sniffing him from his paws to the white tip of his tail. When he showed no reaction, Maple must have decided he was a friend not a foe, and he snuggled against Whiskey's side and they napped together.

Candace declared it "the cutest thing."

"Hey, do you have time for a nail clip?" Candace asked.

"Of course." Sarah took the tan bundle of fur from her friend and placed the rabbit on the counter, holding it in place.

Emily handed over the clippers and stood on the other side of the counter, petting the rabbit, and making soothing sounds. "We'll make it quick, Maple. We promise."

Maple seemed to trust them, though he did try to pull his back foot from Sarah's grasp. In five minutes, they were done and Maple was cradled safely back against Candace's chest. "You guys are the best," Candace said, handing payment to Sarah.

"He made it easy," Sarah said.

"I heard Jared's getting released today," Candace said.

"Yes. I told him I'd pick him up. Do you know what made the big rig driver lose control and hit the library?"

"Not yet. His family has agreed to an autopsy. They'll do a tox screen to make sure he wasn't drunk or high."

Emily piped up, "That whole situation was insane. I'm so glad Jared or anyone we know wasn't killed."

"That was basically a miracle," Candace said. "The Parks thought the driver may have had a heart attack or stroke, but right now that's just speculation until the autopsy results come in so don't spread that around. They doubted the accident caused his death based on the shape he was in."

Sarah frowned like she was in thought before she said, "He had a gash on his head that I saw, but come to think of it, it didn't bleed as much as a head wound often does. I saw Jared in the ER last night. I was surprised how much he joked around and was basically normal after all of that trauma. Just seeing it made me want to crawl into the fetal position and cry like a baby." Sarah tried to remove the images flashing through her mind by shaking her head as if her mind worked like an Etch-a-Sketch.

"Like I said, it could have been much, much worse," Candace quietly reminded.

Emily added, "And I'm sure you've seen it."

Candace nodded her head once. "Well, I've gotta run. Thank you both for clipping Maple's nails. My carpet and drapes thank you too, as he's gotten a bit stuck in them."

"Any time,' Sarah said.

As Candace exited the Coiffure, she held the door open for Daphne Smith and her French bulldog Pierre. "*Merci,* Candace. *Bonjour,* Sarah. *Bonjour,* Emily." Daphne was born and raised in Cottageville and had never been to France, or even to Quebec or Montreal, but she had been taking French lessons from Sarah's next door neighbor Janice Jenkins. Daphne adored all things French from the food to the wine to the language to the scarves. Today, she had a luxurious silk scarf tied around the neck of a black turtleneck sweater dress, underneath her long black cashmere coat. Despite the windy weather, her coat was open as if the inside of her car had been too hot for her coat to stay buttoned.

Emily took Pierre from Daphne's outstretched arms. "Our bows today are either red, green, gold, or silver, for the holidays. Which do you prefer?"

"*Or, merci,*" Daphne said.

"Gold it is," Emily said, carrying Pierre toward a tub and then placing him inside. Whiskey ran under the counter to join them. He stood on his hind legs and placed his front paws on Pierre's tub, and gave his small friend a slurp on his cheek.

Daphne chuckled. *"Amour, très magnifique."*

Sarah said, "Daphne, is lunch time good to pick him up?"

"Oui. Merci." And with that, Daphne turned on her black leather, wooden heeled boots and left the Coiffure.

Sarah lifted up the part of the front counter where it was hinged and walked into the back area, which was a converted kitchen from when the building had been a house. As she did so, the phone in her apron pocket rang. The number was not one she knew.

"Hello? This is Sarah."

"Good morning, mi'lady," Jared said. "They said I will be discharged in thirty to forty minutes. Are you still able to come get me? And does your offer still stand, now that you've had time to sleep on it?"

Sarah heard the smile in his voice. "I'll go home to get the Jeep and I'll see you in a half an hour. And yes, of course, the offer still stands. I even changed the sheets on the guest bed last night."

"Thank you. See you soon."

Sarah disconnected and looked at their schedule to ensure she wasn't leaving Emily in a lurch. The next dog wasn't due for an hour and it was another small one, their favorite corgi named Coco Chanel, who would be accompanied by her very attractive human Braidington Bagley. Sarah smiled to herself as she thought about racing back to the Coiffure in time to see the eye candy.

And that thought reminded Sarah that she and Emily never finished their discussion of the mobile grooming van or the pop-up candy shop. "I need to run home for my car and then go get Jared, but

I just remembered we were talking about the van and the candy store when Candace walked in. Have you been to the candy store?"

Emily sudsed Pierre and said, "Yeah. Travis and I checked it out last week. They have killer old school stuff like Fire Balls and Gobstoppers, in addition to chocolate reindeer and chocolate reindeer poop, candy canes, truffles, and holiday novelty items."

"Huh," Sarah said. "I'll have to check it out. You'll be okay for an hour or two? I'm gonna go get Jared and then we'll run to his place to grab some of his stuff. He's gonna stay with me for a few days until he's a bit more healed. I didn't think it was wise for him to be alone."

"That's probably smart," Emily said. Then she grinned at Sarah like she was holding back a snarky comment.

"What?" Sarah demanded.

Emily grinned bigger. "Nothing."

Sarah rolled her eyes and took off her apron and hung it on a hook on the wall. "I've gotta go. Come on, Whiskey." Sarah wrapped her scarf around her neck and zipped her coat as she opened the counter and went through.

Whiskey walked to the door as if he understood they were leaving.

"You're taking him to the hospital?"

"He can wait in the car. I shouldn't be long. And you know how much he loves Jared."

"That's true. Drive safely. I've got things covered, no problem."

Sarah and Whiskey kept their heads down as they fought against the brisk wind as they traveled up the sidewalk. Soft snowflakes swirled in the breeze and dotted Whiskey's red and white fur.

"At least this doesn't look like it will accumulate," Sarah said to Whiskey as she pulled her scarf tighter around her neck.

He glanced up at her acknowledging that she spoke.

"Come on, boy," Sarah said, breaking into a jog. She ran up Main Street and veered right onto the park path. Whiskey kept pace with her and never left her side. The snow stopped as they approached the children's playground equipment, which was a ghost town on this early December day. The green grass of the park was lightly dusted with snow but it seemed to be melting into the earth as the sun burst through the steely sky. Sarah slowed to a walk and held her face toward the sun, soaking up as much vitamin D as she could.

When they got to their house, Sarah went inside only to grab the keys to her old Jeep. She unlocked the driver's side door and told Whiskey, "Hop in the back." He leapt onto her seat and then through the narrow gap between driver's and passenger's seats onto the back bench seat, and then he sat up and gazed at her through the closed window. She smiled at him, then slid under the steering wheel and shut her door. The Jeep was a gift from Sarah's grandfather, and despite the vehicle's age, its engine turned over on the first try.

Five minutes later, Sarah and Whiskey pulled up the driveway to the front of the ER. Jared peered at them through the automatic sliding glass doors. He was sitting in a wheelchair. A male orderly with curly black hair and wearing blue-gray scrubs held the handles on the chair's back. Lengthwise, crutches rested atop the wheelchair's armrests. Jared had one forearm resting over them and his fingers wrapped around the hand grips to keep the crutches in place. Jared's face lit from within at the sight of Sarah's Jeep. He said something over his shoulder to the orderly, which caused the man to smile. The doors gaped open like a welcoming mouth, and Jared was pushed toward the CJ's passenger side.

Sarah jumped down from the driver's side and ran around the back. "Hey, how are you doing?" she asked Jared.

She realized he was wearing the paint splattered buffalo check plaid flannel and jeans he had on when he came to the hospital. "Oh. I should have thought of bringing you other clothes." She opened the passenger door. Whiskey popped between the two front seats to get a better look at his friend.

Jared shook his head in response to Sarah's clothes comment, as the orderly supported Jared as he stood, and then the orderly handed him the crutches one by one. Jared hopped on his good foot to cover the eight inches of distance between him and his ride. He used the crutches to leverage his butt up into the seat.

Sarah helped him get the crutches into the space next to his seat. Then Jared clicked his seat belt.

The orderly asked if he had everything he came in with.

"And then some," Jared said. "I've added a cast and crutches to my belongings. Thank you. I'm good, captain." He gave the man a two-finger salute.

Sarah said, "I'm so glad the truck didn't squeeze your sense of humor from you."

"It's not toothpaste, Sarah." Jared grinned at her like a crazed jack-o-lantern, as she shut his door and wondered exactly how many meds he was on.

She jogged around the back of the vehicle and got behind the wheel. "So, we'll go grab your stuff from your place and then go to mine."

"Sounds like a solid plan." He leaned the back of his head against the rest and closed his eyes.

"Um, before you zone out, Jared, can you please tell me where I'm going? I mean, I know the general direction, but I've never been to your place," Sarah said.

"Oh yeah, right," Jared said, before he mumbled an address.

CHAPTER SIX

Jared's apartment sat on the outskirts of the south end of town and was atop his landlord's four-car garage. Fifteen wooden steps needed to be climbed to reach the front deck and door. Sarah's eyes widened when she realized the predicament those stairs could cause. "Umm, Jared..." she said, as she eyed the stairs and turned off the Jeep's engine.

"If you can help me to get to them, I think the best way to climb them is on my butt."

"Umm, okay," Sarah said, sure the skepticism seeped from her voice. She ran around to his side of the car, and held onto his arm and the crutches as he pushed himself from the seat onto his good leg. She steadied him as he stepped onto the blacktop. Sarah said a quick prayer of thanks that no snow or ice was on the ground.

Using the crutches, Jared hobbled to the staircase and then turned and parked his butt on the third stair from the bottom. Whiskey stood next to him and slurped the side of Jared's stubbly face. Jared laughed.

"Whiskey, get down here," Sarah said. "I know you want to help but you could be a hindrance. And that's what we don't need right now."

Whiskey hopped down the stairs and stood next to Sarah, facing Jared and the staircase.

"I'm gonna spot you from here," Sarah said, "and make sure you don't fall."

"Yeah, about that. If I fall down the stairs, you'll go down like a bowling pin. Trust me on that. I'd rather you and Whiskey climb up past me and wait at the top."

"But how's that going to stop you from falling?"

"It isn't, Sarah. But at least there won't be two of us in the ER."

"Ahh, okay. Come on, boy." Sarah dropped a kiss atop Jared's head as she and Whiskey climbed past him. And they watched and waited while Jared used his hands and good leg to ascend the stairs from a sitting position, one riser at a time. When he made it to the top, Sarah reached under his arms and pulled him backward on the deck so he was clear of the stairs, before she helped him stand. She used his key to open the door to his place.

They entered into an open plan living room and kitchen. Whiskey ran quickly through the rooms, his nose to the carpet, sniffing. A brown leather sofa sat as a sentinel against one wall with a flat panel television opposite it. End tables flanked each end of the sofa, and atop both were the most exquisite lamps Sarah had ever seen. She approached one as if she were iron and it was magnetic. The base was a hunk of wood inlaid with turquoise and the shade was copper, burnished into the colors of a desert sunset—sky bluish-teal at the bottom with agave shaped cut outs to let through light to blues and purples, hot pink, peach, a wash of blue-gray, and a cutout sun at the top. Sarah traced the cutouts and gradients of color with her index finger. "Wow. I love this," she said.

"Me, too." Jared hobbled toward her on his crutches. "I'll just be a minute. Feel free to explore." He maneuvered himself down the hallway.

Sarah wandered around the well-appointed kitchen, smiling at the red stand mixer and the high-end espresso machine, before she walked through the living room to the hall. The first room on her left looked like a big closet with a window, which Jared clearly used as his studio. A drafting table and stool took up most of the room and on the table was an array of drawings in various stages of shading and coloring. Sarah smiled at the organized clutter, especially when she saw a pencil drawing of the Christmas image Jared promised to paint on the Coiffure's front door. The rendering of Whiskey was so realistic, Sarah's heart felt like it grew three sizes, like at the end of *The Grinch*. She stroked the graphite fur with two fingertips.

She blinked back tears and left the studio. Further down the hall and on the right was Jared's bathroom: white toilet with the lid down, glass shower, white sink, blue towels. Standard. What wasn't standard was the framed black and white photograph of a chimpanzee in a bathtub. Sarah laughed aloud when she spied that above the toilet.

The last door off the hall led to Jared's bedroom. He stood on his good leg next to the bed, while Whiskey sat atop the navy blue comforter, supervising the packing. A black duffle bag lay next to Whiskey, and Jared was pulling clothes from his dresser and stuffing sweatpants, sweatshirts and one sweater, two pairs of balled gray socks, and black boxer briefs into the bag. He asked Sarah to grab his toothbrush, deodorant, and electric razor from the bathroom, and she quickly returned with them.

"Anything else?"

"That book on my nightstand."

"Any art supplies?"

He smiled at her. "Mi'lady, you know me well. We'll grab my sketchbook on the way past the studio."

"Sounds good." Sarah zipped his duffle bag and threw it over her shoulder to his protests. "No. Really, I'll carry it. You focus on those crutches. You don't need the extra weight." Whiskey zipped past them toward the front door. Sarah followed Jared down the hall and waited when he went into his studio for his supplies. She unzipped the bag and let him add his pencils, sketchbook, and laptop to the duffle bag. And then she helped him into his winter coat by holding it for him one arm at a time.

"Just like my mum used to do for toddler-me," Jared joked.

After they locked his front door, Sarah asked Jared to stay on his deck while she took his bag and Whiskey down to the car. Whiskey hopped in the backseat but watched out the window at his friend. Sarah jogged back up the steps and helped Jared sit at the top of the stairs. "Hold onto the rails and take them one at a time," she said, taking the crutches from Jared. "You've got this."

Jared's cast stuck out into the air and with his hands and his good leg, he managed to bump his way down the stairs on his butt. When his good foot was on the ground, Sarah stepped around him and stood in front of him with the crutches planted on both sides of his legs. Jared used the railing to pull himself to standing and took the crutches from Sarah.

She kept her hands out on either side of him as she walked behind him toward the CJ. Then she helped him get into the passenger seat, waited until he got buckled, and then handed him the crutches to hold. Whiskey popped between the front seats and kissed Jared's left cheek, as if he was saying, "Good job."

Jared chuckled. "Thanks, Whisk."

Sarah started the engine as Jared said, "To your castle, mi'lady."

"As you wish, my lord."

Ten minutes of silence later—during most of which Jared sat with his eyes closed—they pulled into Sarah's driveway. When she opened her car door to step out, Whiskey flew past her like Superman on his way to save the world. Except Whiskey was impatient because he had to pee. As soon as his feet hit the grass, he lifted his leg and grinned.

Sarah shook her head. "You're hilarious, dog."

He barked once in agreement.

Sarah grabbed the duffle bag from the floor behind her seat and went around to the passenger side, but Jared was already out of the Jeep and moving his crutches into place so they could be used. Sarah shut the passenger door and then walked ahead of him so she could open the front door before he got to it.

Sarah placed Jared's duffle on the white duvet in her guestroom as

Jared followed her into the room. He said, "Sarah, would it be possible for me to take a bath before you go? I'll be quick, I promise. I'd prefer a shower but the doc said I can't get the cast wet so I figured sitting in the tub with this leg over the edge might be easier. I smell like antiseptic, hospital, and accident."

"Of course you can take a bath. Do you want bubbles? I can start the water."

Jared grinned. "No bubbles. And I can start the water myself. My hands still work fine." He wiggled his sliced up fingers at her like a sea anemone's tentacles moved in an ocean current before he hobbled into the bathroom attached to the guest room.

Sarah called after him as he was shutting the door, "I put fresh towels out for you and there's body wash and a new bar of soap and some shampoo. I'll be out here. Yell if you need help. Please be careful, Jared."

She didn't wait for a reply before she went into the kitchen to make sure Whiskey had water in his bowl. Sarah had decided to leave him home with Jared for the afternoon. While she waited for Jared to finish bathing, she built a turkey and swiss sandwich on rye bread and plated it with a dill spear and a side of potato chips. She wanted to make lunch and life as easy as she could for Jared.

Whiskey barked once from the back door, his signal that he needed to go out.

As Sarah opened the door for him she said, "Whiskey, get your business over with now. I know sometimes you like to be let out and back in over and over while you play with the squirrels and Mozart, but Jared's not up to that." Mozart was a neighbor's cat who arrived almost daily to tease the red heeler.

Whiskey cocked his head to the side, eying her, and then he smiled. He romped into the backyard, sniffed a hibernating azalea and then peed on it, before racing around the side of the house. Despite the chilly air, Sarah jogged down the back steps and into the yard so she could spy what he was up to. His back was to her and he was mid squat. "Good boy," she said as he turned and ran toward her.

Sarah handed Whiskey a dehydrated chicken breast treat just as Jared opened the guest bedroom door. His hair was wet, and he had one gray sweatpants leg gathered up above his cast while the other reached his ankle. "I feel so much better now," he said.

"I made some food in case you are hungry. I need to get back to work, but feel free to help yourself to anything. Nurse Whiskey will be here to supervise."

Jared chuckled. "And he takes bones instead of Blue Shield?"

"Exactly. Call me if you need me. Oh wait. You don't have a phone." Sarah frowned.

"I can iMessage you, from my computer."

"Good thinking." Sarah donned her winter coat, patted Whiskey's head, and gave Jared a hug on her way out the door. She jogged up her street and across the park, before slowing to a walk down Main Street. As she turned left onto the Coiffure's street, she watched the white Moe's Mobile Grooming van creep past her business. *A tortoise moves faster than that van,* Sarah thought. She frowned. *Was the driver spying on her business?* She couldn't see the driver's face, but she was almost certain the cowboy hat was the same worn by the stranger in Java and Juice.

When she closed the front door, she found Coco Chanel was in the wash tub and her gorgeous human had dropped her off. Three big boxes were piled on the counter like FedEx had recently delivered. Sarah eyed the label on the cardboard before realizing that was the rest of the merchandise for the Winter Wonderland. Last week she had decided they didn't have enough stuff so she added dog parkas and dog sweaters in a variety of sizes as well as a few cute Santa, Mrs. Claus, and elf costumes, and some plush reindeer antlers.

"Everything go okay?" Emily asked as Sarah slipped the loop of her apron over her head.

"Yes. Everything is fine. Do you know what time the candy pop-up closes each day? I thought maybe I'd check it out and get Jared a treat."

"I think eight or nine." Emily worked her fingers into the corgi's fur. Coco Chanel closed her eyes and sighed like she enjoyed the massage. "Taylor stopped by Java and Juice while you were gone. Ginger hired him on the spot. She put him in charge of plating or bagging orders and refilling the display cases until after they close today. Then she said she'll train him on the register."

"I hope he's a quick learner. She needs one right now. Hey, are you okay finishing Ms. Chanel?"

"Of course. Do you want candy now?" Emily raised one black eyebrow at Sarah.

"No. I was thinking I'd eat my salad now so I could be done and ready for when Sebastian the St. Bernard gets here. I'll wash him and then you can wash and groom Ming-Chi when she arrives later this afternoon."

"Ooo, that Pekinese is so sweet. I'm glad she's on a regular schedule now. Remember when she first came to us? Boy was she a mess of matts."

"So true." Sarah pulled her salad from the fridge and ran tap water into a glass. She put her phone on the table next to her and looked to see if Jared had sent a message. Then she remembered she had forgotten to check with John Beams if they had found Jared's phone. She sent a short text.

Three dots appeared instantly followed by "Found parts that may have been a phone. Tell Jared I'm sorry."

"Thank you." Sarah wondered if AppleCare provided annihilation coverage. She sent an iMessage to Jared asking if he had AppleCare or renters' insurance. One or the other might cover the cost of a new phone.

The bell tinkled over the front door of the Coiffure as it opened. Salt and pepper haired Hank Silva entered wearing a winter coat paired with postal uniform shorts, knee high black socks, and lace-up boots.

"Aren't your legs freezing?" Emily asked as she lifted a towel-wrapped Coco Chanel from the washtub.

"Nah, I'm used to it." Hank flashed Emily a closed mouth smile. He put their mail on the counter. "Have a great afternoon," he said before leaving the Coiffure.

Sarah swallowed a bite of salmon before walking to the counter to get the mail: six envelopes that could contain Christmas cards and one legal size white envelope with Sarah's name and the Coiffure's address typed on the front. The return address was the mayor's office.

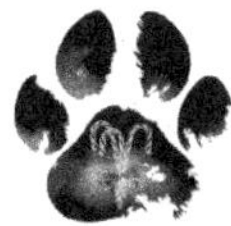

CHAPTER SEVEN

Sarah opened the legal envelope first and her eyes widened when she read the one-page letter on official letterhead that was within. "Hey, Em, listen to this: 'Dear Sarah, It is with great honor that I am naming you Cottageville Citizen of the Year this Friday evening at the kick-off of Winter Wonderland. Please be sure to attend the opening ceremonies at 6 p.m., where I will personally thank you for the crimes you've helped solve and give you a gift as well as symbolic keys to the city. Confirm your attendance by calling my assistant. I look forward to seeing you then. Sincerely, Trish McGowan.' Holy crap!"

"Holy crap is right. But you so deserve it, Sarah."

"Thank you, but I couldn't have solved the last three mysteries if it wasn't for your help and all of our friends."

"And Whiskey." Emily's eyes sparkled as she grinned at Sarah, but before Sarah could agree, Emily fired up the hair dryer and aimed it at Coco Chanel's long back. She ran a brush over the dog as she blew her dry, while murmuring, "Such a beautiful girl. Yes, you are. You're a beautiful girl."

Coco turned her head to eye Emily, and the dog smiled as if she appreciated the compliments.

Sarah opened the Christmas cards one by one. Many had dogs in various moments of holiday cheer: two pugs in front of a decorated tree, a Golden Retriever holding a stocking in his mouth, a black Lab in a Santa suit complete with a snowy white beard under his chin, and a cartoon dog peeing a yellow angel into a snowbank. Sarah added those cards to the others that were taped around the front window's white wooden frame. As she placed the last one, she saw Sebastian and his human Scott Simon pull up in a black Explorer. Sebastian rode shotgun and Sarah was grateful to see the dog was wearing a seat harness. Too many dogs who weren't belted turned into projectiles during traffic accidents. She waved at them through the window and knew Whiskey would be disappointed to miss seeing one of his friends.

"Hey, Sarah," Scott said as he followed Sebastian through the Coiffure's door. Scott wore a zipped-up forest green puffy jacket with his dark jeans and cigar colored Blunstone boots. His salt and pepper hair curled every which way like Kerry blue terrier.

"Hi, Scott. How are you and Sebastian today?" Sarah reached for Sebastian's leash.

"We're great. But how are you? How's business?" Scott eyed her with a look of concern.

"I'm well. Business has been steady." Sarah met his gaze. "Why?"

"Have you noticed that white van around that has Moe's Mobile Grooming on it?"

Sarah nodded her head. "Yeah, I saw it outside of Java and Juice yesterday and then driving past the Coiffure today."

"He's been all over town for the last month, and he's been handing out cards offering a free nail clip to try his service. I thought maybe that would hurt your business." Scott's eyes crinkled and he looked genuinely concerned.

"It hasn't seemed to," Sarah said.

"That's great. Well, I need to go. May I pick him up in two hours?"

"Of course," Sarah said. "And thanks for the heads up on the competition."

"I hope he doesn't provide much," Scott said before he stepped outside.

As soon as the door was shut Emily said, "If that new guy wants to clip Chutney's nails or groom the unholy terror, he's welcome to."

Sarah chuckled. "He's definitely our most problematic client. But it would be better not to lose any of our regulars." She led Sebastian into the walk-in tub, took off his collar, and started the water. Sebastian shook as soon as the warm water touched his fur, which sprayed it in a five-foot radius. "Dude, please don't shake again until we are done." She moved the hose around his body and then turned the water off and worked the suds into his double layer of fur. As she leaned over him, he slurped her upside the face with his giant pink tongue.

"I love you, too," Sarah said, laughing.

The afternoon passed quickly between the grooming appointments, unpacking and inventorying the items in the boxes from FedEx, RSVPing to the mayor's invitation, and messaging with Jared, who let Sarah know that AppleCare+ would indeed replace his phone. A new one was scheduled to be delivered to Sarah's home tomorrow. He hoped she didn't mind.

"Not at all," she responded, just as the Coiffure's green door opened and Robert Wise, a neighbor on Sarah's street, entered her business for the first time. Robert taught music at the high school and he lived with the cat Mozart that sometimes tormented Whiskey. Robert held a black soft sided pet carrier in front of him and the sound that emanated was far from music. Mozart sounded like a creaky door that won't fully close; his vocalizations were low, long, drawn-out, and filled with a sense of longing for freedom from his captivity.

Robert raised his voice to be heard over his frustrated feline. "I came home from work to find the Christmas tree lying on its side, branches broken, and sticky sap everywhere including matting his fur. Please tell me you have something that removes sap from a cat."

"We use mineral oil," Sarah said. "Has he ever had a bath?"

"Every so often. He likes water and sometimes sticks his paw in my shower to play or under the bathroom sink spigot."

"Good. Then we will get the sap out and bathe him. Would you like to help by soothing him as we work since he's not been here before?"

"My pleasure." He handed the carrier to Sarah who opened the counter and walked through while Robert removed his winter coat and set it on a chair in the entryway.

Emily pulled the mineral oil, a wide-tooth comb, and paper towels from the cabinet and two sets of thin black surgical gloves from the top drawer.

Sarah set the cat carrier on a metal grooming table and unzipped the top just enough for Mozart to pop his head up like a periscope. Emily approached with the tools they would need as Robert scratched the top of Mozart's head and started humming and then singing Neil Diamond's "Song Sung Blue". Mozart's eyes twitched as if he were listening and he released a soft mewl.

Sarah opened the carrier fully and picked up the cat, her hands instantly becoming tacky as her finger connected with the tree sap. "That's a good boy," she cooed, as Emily moved the carrier to the floor so she could set the cat back on the table.

Since Emily's hands were already encased in latex, she conducted the first inspection of Mozart's fur as Robert sang and petted the cat's head and Sarah donned gloves. "It's not confined to one area," Emily announced. "Little bits here and there. Fortunately, it hasn't had time to harden."

Sarah opened the oil and poured some onto the sappy spot closest to her and then massaged the mineral oil into Mozart's fur. Emily used the bottle on her side of the cat and back and forth they traded off until much of Mozart was flattened, greasy fur, except for his ears and face, which wore a look of misery. Robert kept up the petting and singing, assuring his boy everything would be alright.

Sarah started the second part of the treatment and ran the comb through the cat's fur starting from his neck to his tail in small strokes, wiping the comb on a paper towel as she went to remove the oil and sap from the tines. It was slow going but effective. Then she handed Mozart off to Emily for his bath.

Unlike many cats, Mozart didn't scream when the warm water hit his body. His face relaxed, his eyes closed, and he let loose a sigh, which caused Sarah to smile.

Robert had stopped his singing. "I can't thank you enough. You guys are lifesavers."

"Was your tree decorated? Is your living room a mess?"

"I put the tree up last night and planned to decorate it tonight. I may have to start over and buy a new tree."

"Might I suggest a sap-less variety such as a reusable tree? They make lifelike ones now or you could go all silver foil or white plastic retro." Sarah grinned at Robert. "I even saw a hot pink one on Etsy."

"Hot pink isn't exactly our color, but I could get into a retro tree."

Sarah thought it would certainly fit some of the music she heard streaming from Robert's windows during the summer months: Streisand, Manilow, Bennett, for example, singers and songwriters Gigi preferred.

"I know that organizations like PETA say to get a smaller fake tree if you have a cat, to put it in a very sturdy, weighted base, to keep the tree away from launch zones or places where they can jump off furniture onto the tree, and to avoid dangly shiny ornaments and tinsel that encourage cats to play. I think those metal hangers for ornaments could be dangerous too so maybe tie ornaments on with string. I don't think you can keep Mozart from being curious or from trying to play with the new toys suddenly in his domain. Whiskey is interested and suspicious of the tree as soon as I put it up, but his interest wanes after the first hour. And he hasn't tried to pee on it since he was a puppy so I consider that a win." Sarah grinned and slipped her apron over her head and hung it on the hook.

Emily had Mozart back on the table and she and Robert cooed at him as she started the blow dryer. Ten more minutes and they'd be done and could close the Coiffure. Sarah refilled the bottles of shampoo, threw the day's assortment of towels from the washer into the dryer, and straightened up in preparation for Thursday.

When Mozart was fluffy, dry, and content to be back in his carrier, Robert paid and thanked them again for helping his muse. After he left Emily audibly exhaled, "What an ending to this day!"

"At least Mozart was pleasant and seemed to understand we were trying to help him. Hey, I'm going to that pop-up candy store. Want to come with me and I'll buy you a treat too for all of your hard work?"

"I'd never say no to candy." Emily removed her apron, grabbed her backpack from the back room, zipped up her black ski parka, and headed toward the door.

Sarah locked up and they walked the short block to Main Street and then crossed over to the storefront. A hot pink neon tube sign in the window declared: WHERE SANTA SHOPS FOR SWEETS. As soon as she opened the glass door, she caught the opening of "We Wish You a Merry Christmas" and the scent transported Sarah to The Chocolate Factory and she expected to see Oompa Loompas. Instead, farmstand bushel baskets like those used by apple orchards topped forest green cloth-covered tables. Every basket was filled to the top with treats and small chalkboard slates attached to two dowels each peeked atop the offerings and let customers know what was in each basket. Sarah looked closer at one and noticed a peanut shell drawn in the bottom right corner. She wondered if that's how the proprietor warned customers of allergens.

"Everything looks so yummy," Sarah said to Emily, who was inspecting a colorful chocolate stocking.

"Yep. And this feels solid, not hollow." Emily carried the stocking with her to the next table. "Ooooo, Pop Rocks. Wasn't there an urban legend about some kid mixing these and pop and his stomach exploded?"

"Yeah. I heard that too. But I don't think it is true." Sarah glanced around the store. They were the only two customers and she didn't see the owner. She wandered from table to table trying to decide what to get Jared. In some ways it was like a multiple choice test with too many answers and most of them seemed correct. She wondered what it would cost if she bought one of everything and then chuckled to herself at how frivolous that would be.

"Know what you want?" Sarah asked Emily.

"You can get me this chocolate stocking. I'm going to buy a few packages of these fancy marshmallows as gifts. What'd you pick out for Jared?"

"Nothing yet. Where are those marshmallows? Are they flavored?"

"Yes, some are and there are dark and milk chocolate covered ones, too." Emily pointed to a table against the wall. "You know he'd love the reindeer poop. Oh, and over by the register she has a basket of hand painted chocolate naughty elves. Travis and I almost peed ourselves laughing at those."

Sarah carried bags of reindeer poop, a few naughty elves, an assorted variety of bags of marshmallows, a couple of six-inch tall chocolate Santas, and a selection of FireBalls, Pop Rocks, and mint-flavored kisses to the register. But there was still no sign of the shop owner.

Emily added her stocking to Sarah's pile.

"Yoohoo, anybody here?" Sarah hollered toward the backroom.

Only the sound of Madonna singing "Santa Baby" answered.

"Maybe she stepped out or is in the bathroom?" Emily suggested.

"Possibly." Sarah shifted her weight from one foot to the other. She eyed the swinging door to the backroom and questioned if she should stick her head back there. She looked down at her watch. It had been at least ten minutes since they left the Coiffure. "Yoohoo," she called again and strained her ears listening for a response that didn't seem to come.

"I'm going to check the backroom," Sarah said. "Stay here."

"Okay," Emily said.

Sarah crossed the eight feet to the hinged stockroom door and pushed it opened with her right hand. She took one step into the room and yelled, "Oh no. Em, call 9-1-1," before racing into the room. A woman lay sprawled on the concrete floor. Her jeans-covered legs were bent at the knees to her left and her arms were motionless at her sides. Her eyes were closed. Blood seeped from behind her head and pooled near her right ear. It matted her chestnut hair.

Sarah knelt next to the woman and reached for her wrist. A pulse beat weakly against Sarah's pointer and middle fingers. She whooshed out a breath of relief. She held the woman's hand and said, "I'm Sarah.

I'm here with my friend Emily and she's calling the medics. We are getting you help."

The woman's eyes did not open and she didn't make a sound.

"Stay with me. Okay? We're going to get through this."

CHAPTER EIGHT

Emily came through the stockroom door with her phone against her ear. "They want to know what the nature of the emergency is." Sarah looked up at her assistant and was about to reply when she noticed Emily's eyes bug bigger than a pug's. "Never mind," Emily mumbled. As she turned to skedaddle from the room, Sarah heard her say, "The candy store owner has collapsed and it looks like she hit her head. There's a lot of blood."

Sarah rubbed the woman's cold hand with her fingers. "Help will be here soon." Sarah's eyes searched the space for something to staunch the blood flow. Other than a few stacked cardboard boxes, the backroom was fairly empty. In one corner was a partitioned space with a door, which Sarah assumed was a bathroom. She didn't want to leave the woman's side to go investigate.

From inside the shop itself, Sarah suddenly heard a rumbling of voices. The stockroom door swung open and Officer John Beams' wide stride in his black boots crossed quickly to Sarah. His black hair curled from under his cop cap. "Sarah," he acknowledged with a nod of his head.

Before Sarah said anything, the door again swung open as a stretcher was pushed through by Wendy Parks, followed by Walter hefting a red paramedic bag. "What have we got?" Wendy asked John.

"Don't know. Just got here myself. Sarah?" Officer Beams pulled a small notebook and pen from his breast pocket.

Sarah let go of the woman's hand, stood, and took a few steps away so Wendy and Walter could do their thing.

"Em and I came for treats when we closed up for the day and when we were ready to check out and no one came to the register, I opened the door to see if she didn't know we were here or something. And that's when I saw her and had Em call you guys."

"Has she been responsive?"

Sarah shook her head no.

"Was anyone in the store when you got here?"

"No."

Sarah glanced toward the Parks to see them wrapping gauze around the woman's head. She and John watched as they shifted her body onto the gurney and then lifted the bed to just below waist level. John speedwalked to the swinging door and held it open as they pushed the litter into the shop, where Emily held open the front door.

Within a minute, they pulled out with their siren wailing, but a split second before they left, the Moe's Mobile Pet Grooming van slammed to a stop against the curb. Stetson man left the van running but stepped down from it, and demanded, "What's going on?"

"Who's asking?" Officer John Beams inquired, positioning himself between the man and Sarah and Emily.

"The owner of this store."

The Parks' van sped down Main Street and Sarah looked from it to the man in the hat.

"Funny," Officer Beams said, "as I thought the owner of this store just left in that ambulance. Now let's start again. What's your name, sir?"

"Maurice Kingsley."

"Got any ID?"

"Of course." Maurice reached behind himself and pulled out a worn, flattened brown leather wallet and extracted his driver's license.

Officer Beams held out his hand for it. "You live in Cedar Rapids."

"Yes. But Fiona and me, we do pop-ups and our other business is mobile." Maurice jerked his arm toward the van, pointing at it with his thumb like he was hitching a ride.

Sarah cringed internally at the improper grammar. She wondered how a mobile grooming business could build a clientele if it didn't stay in one general area. She noticed Emily eying her like she was thinking the same thing.

"Now will you tell me what's going on?" Maurice asked, tapping the toe of his right boot on the sidewalk.

"The woman running the store was found in the backroom in the middle of a medical emergency. The Parks just took her to the hospital."

"What? Is Fiona okay? What happened?" He took off his hat and held it over his heart. His eyes squinted like he was in pain.

"We don't know what happened. These two women—" John pointed behind himself. "Were trying to make a purchase, but no one came to the register. So Sarah went in the back to let the woman, Fiona, you say, know they were there, but she found her collapsed on the floor and they called 9-1-1."

"Oh my God. Was it a heart attack?"

"I don't know. If you have the keys on you, you should probably lock up and go to the hospital. It's nine blocks up Main Street, if you don't know where it is."

"Okay. You're right." Maurice took a few steps toward the store. He stopped and his head bobbed back like all of the candy next to the cash register surprised him. He turned to Sarah and Emily. "Um, if you still want what you picked out, I'll ring you up."

Emily's eyes widened and Sarah said, "Umm, sure, thank you." She, Emily, and John walked back into the store. Sarah mumbled to Emily she'd buy the marshmallow gifts, too, and they could sort it all out later.

After she signed the credit card receipt, Sarah said, "Thank you. I hope Fiona makes a full recovery."

Maurice's dark eyes bore into hers and filled with tears. "Me too."

They waited while Maurice locked the front door, got into his van, and drove north.

"Thanks for the quick thinking, both of you," Officer Beams

said, as he got into his patrol car.

"Of course," Sarah said. "Have a good evening. Come on, Em. I'll walk you back to your car."

After they were again in front of the Coiffure and divvying up the treats, Emily said, "Did you find it weird that in the middle of an emergency, he sold us candy?"

"Kind of. But sometimes shock makes people act strangely. Hey, since I'm already way later than I expected to be home, is there any way you could drop me off at my house?"

"Get in." Emily clicked the unlock button on her key fob.

As they drove up Main Street and then around the park, Emily asked, "Do you think Fiona had a heart attack?"

"I have no idea. Heart attack, aneurysm, stroke, it could have been anything. She could have even fallen and hit her head on the concrete floor. She wasn't conscious."

"It looked like a lot of blood." Emily's voice was almost a whisper.

"Head wounds bleed. It's what they do." Sarah sucked in an audible breath. "I wonder who is going to have to clean that up."

Emily shivered, but said nothing.

"Thanks for the ride home. See you tomorrow, Em. Enjoy the chocolate."

"Thanks, Sarah. Enjoy time with your patient." She giggled.

Whiskey barked in greeting before Sarah opened the front door. "Did you miss me, boy?" He raced past her onto the front lawn and lifted his leg before he nipped back inside. She scratched between his ears before removing her winter jacket. She put the bag of sweets and her house keys on the mission style oak console table by her front door.

"We both missed you," Jared yelled from the living room.

"Wow. Something smells amazing. Sorry I'm late." Sarah and Whiskey walked side by side into the living room. Jared's back was to her, and his casted right leg stretched the length of her sofa. She walked around the furniture so she could make eye contact. "You cooked?"

"Sort of. I had Produce and More deliver some things that could be easily thrown into a dish and baked in the oven. It's been done awhile so it may be a bit dry. But I meant it as a thank-you."

"That's so sweet," Sarah said. "May I plate it and bring it to you? We can eat in here, if it is easiest for you."

"Actually, the table is probably better. I'd hate to get red sauce on your sofa." Jared ran his hand over the gray leather covering a cushion.

"Yeah, I'd hate for that, too." Sarah grinned. "Do you need help getting up?" She eyed Jared's crutches, which were laying like fallen tree branches between the sofa and coffee table.

"Nah. I've got it. Did you have a good afternoon?" Jared swung the cast in a one-legged scissor kick to get it closer to the ground. Then he bent at the waist to retrieve the metal mobility aids.

"My afternoon turned unexpected. Let me get the delicious dinner and I'll tell you about it as we eat. I'll meet you at the table."

"Sounds good." With both hands clutching the grips, Jared launched himself to standing.

"You're getting good at that," Sarah said.

"Just the skill I wanted to acquire," Jared joked as he hobbled toward the dining table in the craftsman bungalow's open floor plan.

Sarah donned potholders with finger pouches before opening the oven door and removing a lidded casserole dish. On two white plates, she scooped chicken, garlic, mushrooms, and assorted veggies with long fettuccine noodles in a red sauce. Her kitchen smelled like the best Italian restaurant. "Hey, did Whiskey have dinner already?"

"He did. I gave him part of a chicken breast when I put our dinner together. That was okay, right?"

"Yes. Thank you."

Sarah grabbed napkins, two forks, and the two plates of food and carried them into the dining room. "What would you like to drink?" She put a plate, one of the napkins, and one of the forks in front of Jared.

"I'm good," Jared said.

"No water? Nothing?"

"Not right now."

"Okay. I figured wine wouldn't mix with your pills."

"Probably not. So, tell me about your day."

"Well, for the second day in a row, it ended with a medical emergency," Sarah started, before launching into the story of wanting to surprise him with a treat from the candy pop-up store.

When she finished, Jared said, "Wow. I hope she's going to be okay. And it's a good thing you found her. Then again, you seem to have a knack for knowing when people need help."

"True." Sarah shrugged and took another bite of food. "This is really good. But you didn't have to do this. It seems like it took a lot of standing to make this happen."

"Not too much. Like I said, I went the easy route. I only had to cut the chicken into pieces, throw it in with the already sliced mushroom and the frozen veggies, add the fresh pasta and sauce, and *voila*. Instant meal while I rested on the couch as it cooked."

"Wow. Thank you so much. And thank you from Whiskey, too. I'm sure he loved his chicken." Sarah swallowed another bite of noodle and then said, "Oh, and I got a letter from the mayor's office today. I'm being given the keys to the city on Friday night at the Winter Wonderland kick-off."

"Really? That's awesome."

"Thank you. Though I couldn't have solved the mysteries this year without you and Whiskey and Em." Sarah grinned at him. "I want you to be there. Can we get you an all-terrain wheelchair or something so you can come with me? It would mean a lot."

Jared held her gaze. "It would mean a lot to me, too, to be your date."

"Then let's figure out a way to make that happen. So, besides getting your phone sorted and making me this beautiful meal, how did you spend your afternoon? Did you rest like the doctor ordered?"

"I did. Whiskey and I curled together in the spare room for more than an hour. He insisted on being the big spoon though it was more like he aligned his spine with mine."

At his name, Whiskey lifted his chin off his paws and tilted his head to let them know he was listening.

"Sometimes the weight of him against me can be too heavy. I hope you know you can push him away or ask him to move if you need some space."

"Nah. He's my best bud. And he's been an attentive nurse. In fact, until you arrived at the front door, he never left my side. Not even when I had to pee." Jared's eyes sparkled like emeralds as he grinned.

"I guess he took my orders of making sure you were safe seriously.

Good to know." Sarah stood and placed Jared's empty plate atop of hers. "I have chocolate and classic candy for dessert. Be right back."

When she returned and emptied the bag of candy sweets onto the table, Jared said, "Ooo, Pop Rocks. I haven't had those since I was five."

"They're all yours," Sarah said. "Eat whatever you want. Though I thought I'd save some of the marshmallows for a decadent hot chocolate the next time it snows."

"Sounds good. May I eat this elf? He's mooning us." The elf did indeed have his green pants pulled past his apricot colored butt cheeks.

Sarah chose another elf who had his middle finger raised in front of his body. "I guess he doesn't like everyone demanding gifts this time of year."

"Or he hates working in the toy factory. Santa probably pays minimum wage. Or are elves slave labor? Hmm." Jared's brow furrowed as he considered the question. "How did Santa hook up with those elves and the reindeer? I mean, I've always taken the stories for granted. Santa, Mrs. Claus, the flying reindeer, those elves, and the North Pole. But elves originally were a part of Norse mythology and were thought to bring illness and rashes and bad dreams to people. How did we jump from there to them making toys and supporting the jolly old soul?"

"Umm, the elves or their union hired an agency and rebranded to a better image?" Sarah ate the elf's stocking feet.

"Very funny," Jared said. "We tell children such weird stories. The Easter Bunny. The tooth fairy. That a stork brings babies. That Santa somehow circumnavigates the globe in only one night and visits everyone on earth." He stared vacantly at the empty cellophane wrapper from the elf he had consumed.

"Would you like some herbal tea?" Sarah asked softly, not wanting to intrude on his thoughts.

He raised his head and his eyes met hers. "Sorry. During the past twenty-four hours I've had too much time to think. Or maybe it's the fact that I could have died yesterday."

Sarah reached for his hand, careful of his cuts. "I'm so glad you didn't."

"Me too. But it puts some things in perspective." He squeezed her hand and then released it.

Sarah waited for him to say more but his mouth was closed like a locked vault, keeping the rest of his thoughts and emotions sealed tightly inside. A few beats passed and then Sarah stood and went into her bedroom and emerged with her laptop. "I'm gonna see where we can rent you a wheelchair for Friday night."

"Or the Parks might know," Jared said. "Do you have their number?"

"No, I don't." She opened her computer and searched Google for "wheelchair rentals near me."

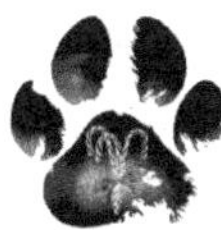

CHAPTER NINE

On Thursday morning's walk, a leash-less Whiskey led Sarah on his usual route, up their street, through the park, and onto Main Street, stopping to snag a treat from Bill, an elderly widower, who even though the temperature was near freezing, sat outside in a sheepskin coat, trapper hat with the flaps up, and gloves, holding his morning coffee. *The Cottageville Courier* was spread on the table in front of him. Bill kept a gallon size glass jar of dog biscuits next to him. Whiskey loved to say hello and get the reward, so he bounded up Bill's front steps and sat at his feet and put out a paw for a handshake.

"Morning, Bill," Sarah called. "Not too cold for you out

here?" She wore a navy puffy jacket, a deep brown wool scarf, and a matching wool beanie. Her hands were jammed into her pockets to avoid frostbite.

Bill shook Whiskey's paw and then handed him a chicken biscuit. "I'm native, Sarah. I've got Iowa winters in my blood." He smiled at her.

"The seasons here certainly beat eight months of Seattle rain. Though last year, my parents somehow ended up with a whiter winter than we did."

"Yes. The weather does seem to be changing. Hey, I heard a rumor you're being honored by Mayor Trish tomorrow night. Did you write a speech?"

"What? No. I don't need a speech. I'm humbled that she thinks my asking questions and snooping around has benefitted Cottageville."

"It sure has," Bill said. "Though I remember when this place was a bit duller, without the kidnapping and attempted murders." Bill grinned as wide as a crescent moon.

"I'll take attempted over accomplished any day. Will you be at the festival?"

"I wouldn't miss it. And besides, Gladys and Janice wouldn't let me even if I wanted to." His eyes sparkled like sunlight dancing on snow.

"I look forward to seeing you there. Have a pleasant day, Bill, and thanks again from Whiskey for the biscuit. Come on, boy, we need to be on our way." Sarah led Whiskey back through the park. Jared had been in his room with the door closed when they left for their morning walk at seven. Sarah wanted to see if he needed anything before she left for work, so she jogged back to her house with Whiskey running alongside her the whole way.

When she opened her front door, the smell of coffee, with notes of toasted nuts and hints of dark chocolate wrapped around Sarah like a comforting blanket. "Wow. Did you bring your own blend?" Sarah asked, hanging her coat in the closet by the door.

"I did indeed, mi'lady," Jared said. He was in navy blue sweats today and his carroty hair stuck out in every direction. Sarah caught a glimpse of his childhood self and she thought he was adorable.

When she entered her kitchen, she curtsied to him. "My lord, how did thou sleep?"

He handed her a black mug of black coffee. "Heavenly. Thank you. I received notification that my new phone should be here before noon so I'll contact the medical device rental places then."

"Sounds good, but I'll also check with Gladys and Janice this morning and see if they know of anyone with one not in use. We saw Bill having his coffee on his porch today, but I forgot all about it. Do you need help with anything before I need to go to the Coiffure?"

"No, thank you. I'm getting around okay with the crutches and I'm going to see if I can last today without the pain meds."

Sarah refilled Whiskey's water bowl. "Does that mean you are feeling okay? I planned to leave Nurse Whiskey here for you again today."

"I'd love the company." Jared took a sip of his coffee. "I noticed a package of ground beef in your freezer. Can I thaw it and make you dinner again tonight? Nothing fancy."

"I could get used to this," Sarah joked. "Need me to pick up anything before I come home?"

"Nah. But if that changes, I'll send you a message."

"Okay. If you get bored, feel free to use my streaming services. If you are asked for a password, it's our zip code."

"I don't think I will. If I have enough energy today, I'm going to work at your table. I have a new graphic novel I'm storyboarding and I was designing a holiday card for Java and Juice and had promised it to Ginger by the weekend."

"I'm sure she'll understand if you need a few more days." Sarah grabbed her go-cup and slid her arms into her jacket. Before she put on her beanie and gloves, she scratched Whiskey, who was lying on the sofa, around his ears. "Take care of Jared for one more day. I love you and will see you later." Then she kissed the top of his head and when she stood again, she was flashed with the black gummed cattle dog grin.

Jared chuckled. "He sure knows how to shine."

"That he does." Sarah walked to her dining table where Jared now sat with his coffee and his laptop. She bent and kissed his cheek. "Take care of yourself. I should be home around five-thirty."

As Sarah walked through the park, she spied Gladys, wrapped up with a long royal blue winter coat and wearing a black knit cap, and her poodles Kahlo and Cassatt, both wearing holiday themed sweaters, near the empty children's playground. Kahlo had her nose to the ground sniffing under a swing. Sarah figured a child must have dropped some food morsels there.

"Good morning, Gladys."

"Good morning, Sarah. Where's your sidekick?"

"Jared's been staying with me since he got out of the hospital yesterday so Whiskey's keeping him company."

"Oh that's nice. Very kind of the both of you."

"You don't happen to know anyone who has a wheelchair they aren't using, do you? Jared wants to come with me to Winter Wonderland, but he doesn't think he can maneuver it well with the crutches."

"Rumor around town is you are being recognized as Cottageville Citizen of the Year so I'm sure he wants to see that. He's sweet on you, you know, dear."

Sarah grinned. "He means a lot to me too, but we are still working things out."

Kahlo finally stopped sniffing and squatted to poop. Sarah took a bag from her jacket pocket and bent to pick up the dog poo so Gladys didn't have to. Gladys thanked her and then said, "I have a wheelchair. It's old and dusty and in my garage. My husband needed it at the end of his life. You are welcome to it. In fact, Janice is picking me up for yoga in an hour. I can have her drive it to your house for Jared."

"Oh wow. That's so kind of you. Thank you."

"Of course, dear. Now, I know you have to get to work, so you have a nice day. And I look forward to seeing you get that award from Mayor Trish. Your grandmother would be so proud. I wish she was still with us to see it." Gladys' eyes teared and she wiped the right one with her glove.

"Thank you, Gladys, it means the world to me that you'll be there since she can't be. I love you." Sarah hugged her and then said good-bye.

Five minutes later as she walked down Main Street she noticed Moe's Mobile Grooming was parked in front of the candy pop-up shop and the lights were on. Maurice, still wearing his hat, moved merchandise from boxes into the bushels. *Hmm,* Sarah thought. She thought they made the chocolates, but maybe they didn't if they were unloading inventory from corrugated boxes. *Would he be manning the store now until Fiona returned? But what about his business?*

Sarah knew it was none of her business what Maurice did. She shook her head to clear her thoughts and went into Java and Juice. Taylor was at the register with a couple of customers in front of him placing their orders. When it was Sarah's turn, his pale face lit in recognition. "Hi, Sarah. Where's Whiskey?"

"He stayed home today to keep Jared company."

Sarah handed Taylor her cup, who in turn handed it to Ginger, who was filling the orders.

"How's he doing?" Ginger asked Sarah, and added to Taylor, "She gets the dark roast with no room for cream."

"Okay," Taylor said, selecting that option but then he paused. "What size?"

Ginger said, "Medium."

"He seems to be doing well. He actually had dinner ready for us when I got home last night. That was nice. And the food was delicious, too. The man can cook." Sarah's eyes crinkled when she smiled.

"Anything else?" Taylor asked.

"Two of the Christmas scones and barbeque chicken salads, if you have any. Oh, and Ginger, Jared said he'd work on your holiday card today as he intends to meet the deadline."

Ginger shook her head causing her blond hair to bounce. "He's the only person I know who won't let being hit by a truck stop him. Taking a few days to rest and heal isn't being idle."

Taylor told Sarah the total and she handed him her credit card. "I know. How much do you want to bet he'll ask you to come back to work part-time next week?"

"I'd never take that bet. It's almost a guarantee." Ginger handed her BFF the bag of food. "I'll meet you at the park tomorrow at three to set up our booth."

"Okay. Have a great day."

"Say hi to Emily for me," Taylor said.

"I will, Taylor." Sarah left Java and Juice pondering how her assistant was juggling dating both Taylor and Travis. *Was she buying them both Christmas presents? And who was she spending the holidays with?* Sarah and Whiskey were invited to Ginger and Daniel's for Christmas, as her parents would be spending Christmas with her brother who was in veterinary school in Scotland. She was pretty sure Jared would be at Ginger and Daniel's, too, though they hadn't discussed it.

Emily was already washing Bug the pug when Sarah strolled through the Coiffure's green door. Bug's big eyes implored Sarah to get Emily to stop. He was a dog who hated baths and being groomed so they saw him infrequently. But his human, Fred, who worked as security at the hospital, had called earlier in the week saying they were going on a road trip to his mother's house in Colorado next week and she insisted Bug "not smell like a dog" when he arrived. Fred joked, "I wouldn't want him to smell like a cat. He is a dog, so I don't know what she expects."

"We'll make sure he smells clean. That's the best we can do. And we can put a bowtie on his collar so she knows he's a proper gentleman," Sarah said.

"Sounds good. Do you have a plaid one for the holidays?"

"Green and black or red and black?"

"Green, please. Thank you, Sarah."

Now, Bug was clearly wishing he were anywhere but at Carter's Canine Coiffure. Sarah put on her denim paw print apron and stood next to the wash tub. "Who's a good boy? You are, Bug. Such a good boy." He strained his neck reaching toward her hand which was moving toward him with a freeze-dried liver treat.

Just then the front door opened and two sable shelties, Sean and Sofia, came in with their heads held high and straining at their leashes, trailed by Sergio, the town's most upscale hairdresser. Sergio was dressed head to toe in fashionable, fitted black, as usual. Even his thick cowhide biker's jacket looked made to order and straight from the latest runway in Milan. "Children, calm down," Sergio commanded though his kids had no intention of following his order.

Sean and Sofia's heads scanned like speed readers as they searched for Whiskey, the Coiffure's official greeter and entertainment.

"He's at home," Sarah said to the shelties.

"What's your salon dog doing at home?" Sergio handed Sarah his dogs' leashes.

"Playing nursemaid to Jared Greene."

"Such a tragedy." Sergio tsked. "How is he? No one makes a better oat milk latte and the things he can draw with foam. Well..."

His voice trailed off.

"He is an *artiste*, that's for sure. He's doing well, all things considered. Sore, cut, and banged up. But has a good outlook, as always. He's staying with me while he recuperates."

"Good. Times like that it sucks to be single." Sergio was notoriously single as the talk around town was that his standards drove most potential partners away. The environment for his employees at his salon was no different. You did things Sergio's way or you didn't work there. But those who could adapt, or ignore him without hurting his feelings, made very good livings as his place was THE place to be cut and colored in a fifty-mile radius.

"Two hours? And bows or bandannas today?" Sarah pulled out the options from a shelf under the counter and Sergio chose the gold lamé bows.

"Two is fine. I'll send Travis. Ta ta for now." He bent and kissed each dog on the top of its head. "Be good for Sarah and Em."

Sarah put Sofia in a tub while Sean sniffed around the floor like a bloodhound on the scent of a long-lost trail, his focus was unwavering, every sense locked onto the target, determined and relentless in the pursuit of something Sarah couldn't see. "We'll just let your brother have at it," Sarah said to Sophia. "Let's make you even more beautiful than you already are."

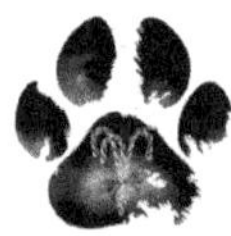

CHAPTER TEN

Eight hours later, Sarah and Emily were done for the day. They were drained and drenched from their last client of the afternoon, a Newfoundland that shook not just once but three different times, spraying water in a six-foot radius from his big and powerful black body. They said good-bye to him and Sarah locked the door behind him. She threw her apron and Emily's and all of the towels they had used into the washer on the quick cycle. And then they refilled the shampoo bottles, swept and mopped the floor, and sanitized all of the surfaces while they waited for the load of laundry to finish.

"Any plans tonight?" Sarah asked Em.

"Studying. Finals are next week." Emily had transferred from the community college to a four-year online program in the fall.

"We only have two clients in the morning. Do you want to take the morning off? I think I can handle it and you've already agreed to work our booth with me tomorrow evening."

"Ooo, that sounds great. Thanks. What time do you need me at the park? Or do you want me to meet you here to pack everything up and unload it?" Emily put away the mop and emptied the bucket as Sarah transferred the items in the washer into the dryer.

"Meet me here at two. We're meeting Ginger at the park at three."

"Okay. Cool. Have a good night, Sarah."

Sarah bundled into her puffy jacket and put on her gloves and hat in preparation for the chilly air. The sun was just starting to set. As Sarah walked up Main Street, she noticed the candy store was closed and its lights were off. The mobile grooming van was nowhere to be seen. She wondered how Fiona was doing, and what, exactly, had caused her to collapse in the backroom. The only person she could think of to ask was John Beams so she texted him. "Just curious if you learned what happened to Fiona. Why did she collapse?"

"Where are you?" Officer Beams responded instantly.

"Walking up Main Street on my way home."

"Meet me on the swings."

Umm, okay, thought Sarah, wondering why he wanted a clandestine meeting instead of texting a response. She hastened her step to a near-jog, and when she crested a small hill, she spied John already on a swing, the toe of his boot planted into the ground, rocking himself from side to side. He was the only one on the playground and the only one besides her in the park, at least as far as Sarah could see.

"Hey," Sarah said by way of greeting as she plunked her butt in the recycled rubber swing next to his.

"What I'm about to say to you is completely off the record. But since you found her, I thought you should know." John's hazel eyes bore into hers.

"Okay—" she dragged the word out.

"The wound on the back of her head was made by a blunt object, not the floor."

"Wait. What?" Sarah's eyes widened.

John nodded his head once and waited for her to process what he had said.

Barely above a whisper, Sarah said, "Someone hit her from behind?"

"That's what we think. It bashed in part of her skull."

Sarah shivered. "A robbery?"

"Don't know."

Sarah shivered again and it had nothing to do with the near-freezing temperatures. What could have happened if she and Emily had been at the store a little earlier? Would they have been attacked too? She squinted at the ground in front of her. Or would they have been able to fend off the attacker?

"I saw Maurice at the store in the early morning. Does he know?"

"I believe so. He was at the hospital last night and again most of today, when the doctor called us to report the finding. He seems very distraught. She hasn't regained consciousness."

"Oh. That's not good." Sarah audibly exhaled.

"No, it isn't."

"Any clue what she was hit with? Did the doc find any fragments?" Sarah knew from watching crime shows and reading mysteries that sometimes doctors or forensic scientists would recover a sliver of wood or a coating from metal or whatever that could then give them clues about the weapon.

"No. Nothing obvious when they cleaned the wound." John used the same toe of his boot to stop his swing from moving.

"So we have no idea if it was a random robbery or if she was intentionally attacked..." Sarah's voice trailed off.

"Or if it was an attempted murder," John filled in the other possible scenario. "So we don't know if we should warn all shop owners or not. But try to make sure you and Em are together at the Coiffure until we know more."

"I will," Sarah said, but then remembered she was scheduled to work on her own tomorrow morning. *Problem solved,* she thought. She'd have Whiskey resume his meet and greet and security guard duties.

"And remember, I've told you all of this in confidence," John reminded.

"I understand. But can I at least tell Em since she was with me when I found Fiona?"

"I'd rather you didn't. It's not that I don't trust Emily, but the least amount of people who know the better. We have a lot of investigating to do and evidence to find. We can't have it possibly tainted if word gets out that we are onto something or someone."

"Makes sense," Sarah said. "Thank you for letting me know. And you know how I like to brainstorm mysteries—"

"We're the police, Sarah. We've appreciated your help in the past. But we've got this covered." John grinned at her and the smile was reflected in the light in his eyes.

"Of course you do," Sarah said. "I"m just saying… Anyway, I've gotta get going. Jared is staying with me while he recovers and I'm late for dinner now. For the second night in a row. Good to see you, John. Too bad it is under these circumstances." Sarah patted his upper arm.

"Goodnight, Sarah. Say hi to Whiskey for me."

Sarah jogged through the rest of the park and down her street to her front door. She knew it would be an internal struggle to keep the secret of what happened to Fiona from Jared and Emily, but she was determined to uphold the promise she made to keep her lips sealed.

Whiskey met her at the door and put his front paws up on her legs and stretched for some scratching of his ears. "Good to see you, too, Whisk," Sarah said.

After hanging up her jacket, she went into the kitchen and greeted Jared. She hugged him hello and relished how warm and solid he felt in her embrace. One against the other, his crutches were propped against the kitchen counter and most of his weight was on his unbroken leg.

"How are you feeling today?" Sarah asked when she pulled back to eye his face.

"Okay. Not awesome. Sore, and the bruises that were deep inside are starting to surface. That makes me look like I went too many rounds with Mike Tyson and definitely lost."

"I'll hug you more gently next time."

"Hugging you doesn't hurt. It makes me feel better. Janice dropped off the wheelchair. Thank you for that. My phone arrived around eleven. Thank God I had everything saved to the cloud. It made set up much easier. And I missed calls and texts from that lawyer, you know the one with the 'Les gets more for his clients' billboards? He wants to represent me when I sue the truck driver or the trucking company or the manufacturer of the truck if it was faulty. Can you believe that?"

"Ambulance chaser. Clearly. Did you tell him to get lost?" Sarah frowned. "Did you get the work done you wanted to do?"

"I told him I was pretty sure it was an accident and I wasn't interested in suing. He argued that I should get my medical bills covered. I told him that's what insurance was for." He shook his head like he was trying to erase the memory of the call. "Anyway, I got some work done. I finished the card for Ginger and sent it to her. But mostly I felt too tired to do much, so Whiskey and I took you up on your offer to binge watch a show and nap. Turns out we are really good at both." Jared smiled.

"That's good. But I think tomorrow I may take him to work again with me, if you can spare him. The customers have been asking about him."

"Yeah, word is getting around that I'm shacked up with you." Jared chuckled. "The gaming group I belong to sent a bunch of texts today, some...umm...congratulating me for, and I quote, 'taking the next step with you finally'—and yes that finally was all in caps—and others razzing me saying you're too good for me." Jared looked sheepish, like a boy caught with his hand in the cookie jar. He tried to hide his embarrassment at admitting his friends' comments behind a nervous smile and lowered eyes.

Sarah's laughter broke the tension like a sudden burst of sunlight through heavy clouds, instantly warming the room and dissolving the tension. "A. It's been fun shacking up with you. B. Umm, I guess we still need to talk about a possible next level. And C, neither of us is too good. Some people...umm...well, some people think we are a perfect match." As she admitted those last nine words she kept her eyes glued to the kitchen floor. Part of her couldn't believe she said them aloud.

She looked up when Jared's arm went around her and pulled her against him.

"I don't know which people you are referring to, but I happen to agree with them." He bent down and placed a soft kiss against her lips. When he pulled back, he added, "So, Sarah Rebecca—that's your middle name, right?—Carter, would you officially be my girlfriend? Uhh, that sounds so middle school. I need a do-over. Sarah, can we be exclusive? There. That sounds more adult. Will you? Can we?"

"Yes, my middle name is Rebecca, and yes, we can be a couple." She raised onto her tiptoes and planted a kiss on his lips that ended up deepening until Whiskey tried to force his way in between both of their legs like he didn't want to be left out.

They broke apart and said "Geez, dog" at the same time.

As they sat at the dining table and ate, Sarah hit the highlights of her day, omitting her meeting with Officer Beams. When Sarah mentioned that she gave Emily the day off and only had two smaller clients in the morning, Jared asked if she could drive to work and he could tag along and sit on a chair and paint the promised painting of

Whiskey with a candy cane in his mouth on the front door. "As much as my body feels like it was hit by a truck…" Jared chuckled to himself. "I think it will be good for me to get back out there and work."

"Uh, does this mean you plan to go back to Java and Juice soon, too?" Sarah raised her eyebrows at him.

"I'll see how I feel after this weekend, but maybe for a few hours a day I could." Jared stacked his silverware on his now-empty plate.

"We knew it." Sarah flashed him a satisfied grin.

"We?"

"Ginger and I discussed that you'd try to come back next week."

"You both know me so well. Clearly, I'd need to sit down on the job. But with a high stool, I could run the register and she and the newb could do everything else."

"Taylor. That's your new co-worker's name. He has an iguana named Iggy that I'm sure you'd like."

"Sounds like a great kids' book character. Or Iggy the iguana could be a new superhero. He already has a built-in fauxhawk."

Sarah shook her head. "You're a nut."

"My sense of humor is as crooked as a cashew." He wiggled his eyebrows at her.

"Oh geez. Being subjected to bad jokes, is that what I agreed to when I agreed to be your girlfriend?" Sarah playfully slapped his arm.

"Absolutely. And you've known me plenty long enough to know what you were committing to."

"Yes. No temporary insanity in my defense."

"Or long-term either," Jared quickly added.

"Anyway, back to the discussion before this craziness started.

Yes, I will drive us—all three of us—to the Coiffure in the morning if you don't mind staying through both of my clients. Then I can drive you and Whiskey home, we can have lunch and relax a little, before I drive back to meet Emily so we can load up the table and boxes and everything we will need for Winter Wonderland for the weekend. Once we are done with the setup, I will leave her and Ginger to man the booth while I come home, change into something less grubby, and pick up you, Whiskey, and the wheelchair, and drive us all back to the park."

"It's going to be so exciting to see you accept the keys from Mayor Trish. And I can yell, 'Yo, that's my girlfriend, everyone,'" Jared joked.

"Uh, yeah, don't. Please don't. While I'm honored to be honored tomorrow night, you know I prefer my personal life to be under the radar. Too many microscopes in this town." As the words left her mouth Sarah wondered if the cops or the docs had used a microscope to look for particulates in Fiona's wound. Could there be a trace of something that couldn't be seen with the naked eye and that didn't wash out when they flushed away the blood? She made a mental note to ask John about that the next time she saw him.

Whiskey interrupted her thoughts by scratching at the back door. As she went to let him out, she said over her shoulder to Jared, "Thank you so much for dinner. I'll clean up. You can return to the couch or wherever and rest if you need to. After I do the dishes and put the leftovers away, I'm going to shower and do some things for tomorrow." One of the things she wanted to do but didn't say was a web search to see if anyone had written about the Cottageville pop-up candy store on social media. Sarah was determined to find out Fiona's last name and anything else that she could about her.

CHAPTER ELEVEN

Friday at five forty-five p.m. Sarah parked the CJ in a small lot on her side of the park. Most citizens walked to the Winter Wonderland, and though the air was cold, it was windless and clear with a starry sky and half-moon shining brightly. The sun had set an hour ago. Sarah pulled the wheelchair from the back of the vehicle, unfolded it, and then wheeled it to Jared's side of the car. Whiskey followed her as he had jumped into her seat as soon as she vacated it and then down to the pavement. Over Jared's forest-green sweatshirt and sweatpants—the leg of his jeans couldn't be pulled over his cast— he wore a navy down jacket and a beanie embroidered with a skeleton doing a skateboard trick.

"Do you want to leave your crutches in the car or take them with us?" Sarah asked.

"In the car is fine." Jared sank into the dark gray vinyl seat of the wheelchair.

Sarah flipped the foot rests down and helped Jared get his cast onto one. She handed him the loop Whiskey's leather leash before she got into position behind the wheelchair, grabbed the handles with her gloved hands, and pushed them to the sidewalk. For its age and disuse, the wheels rotated just fine.

People said hi to them as they passed. Some Sarah didn't know, but they stopped to tell Jared how glad they were he wasn't hurt worse or how great it was to see him. He smiled at everyone, shook hands, and thanked them for their well wishes. He promised to be back to making their lattes and foam art soon.

At five to six, Sarah parked Jared's wheelchair to the left of the temporary stage. Whiskey sat on his butt against the right wheel of the chair. Jared scratched between his ears and murmured, "Good boy." A large golden throne rose majestically from the flooring behind and to the left of the podium and costumed elves bustled about. In half an hour, Santa—played by George, owner of Produce and More—would sit there, become a children's confidant, and pose for photos, doing his annual duties. Mayor Trish and her assistant walked the stage checking the microphone and speaker levels, ensuring everything— the speech, the lighting of the tree, the arrival of Santa—would go off without a hitch. Trish wore an almost ankle length wool coat of the deepest brown over brown leather boots with a braid running down the outside. She had on what looked to Sarah like a cashmere cream beret and matching cashmere gloves. Sarah admired how polished Trish looked, like a Ralph Lauren model, oozing classic American style. Trish flashed a small smile and gave Sarah a nod of her head to acknowledge she saw her. Around and behind Sarah, Jared, and Whiskey their neighbors and strangers started to gather excited for the festivities to begin.

Then Mayor Trish's voice boomed from a too loud microphone. "Good evening, Cottageville citizens and guests. I'm Trish McGowan, mayor of this fine town, the best place, in my opinion, to live and work and play in America."

A cheer and hoots and clapping erupted.

She grinned from the podium and her head turned as she slowly scanned the crowd. She continued, "I thank you all for joining us for Winter Wonderland, for supporting our local businesses, for decorating your homes and engaging in holiday cheer, and for showing goodwill to all of our residents and guests this holiday season. It's been an incredible year for our community. I want to personally thank Chief James Order and his team for keeping us safe and protected."

Another cheer and round of clapping occurred.

"And thank you to Wendy and Walter Parks for the first-rate ambulance service they run. Many people here owe their lives to you, literally. We are in debt and are forever grateful."

The Parks waved to the crowd, and Wendy threw some air kisses, which caused Sarah to grin.

"And now, while I'm thanking people who have served our community this year, I'd like Sarah Carter, owner of Carter's Canine Coiffure, where I know many of you take your pets to be groomed, to come to the stage." Mayor Trish paused and waited while the crowd broke into applause.

Jared grabbed and squeezed her hand before she left his side. Sarah walked up the few steps onto the stage and smiled as she looked out to the faces of the people she loved: the Parks, the Chief with Sascha and Barbara, Gladys, Bill, Mrs. Jenkins, Ginger and Emily in the back, standing at their shared booth, and so many others.

Mayor Trish turned her head toward Sarah as she talked into the microphone. "Many of you know this year has been unique in its challenges. Our usually quiet town had a kidnapping, a con, and attempted murders, and yet we overcame these things by neighbors looking out for each other and from the persistence of this woman right here, Sarah Carter, and her friendly and fabulous cattle dog Whiskey."

At his name, Whiskey strained against his leash and lunged toward the stage. Jared let him go. His ear flattened as he ran full force up the stairs and skidded to a stop next to Sarah and Mayor Trish, who burst out with laughter. "Way to make an entrance, Whiskey," she said. The crowd went wild with cheers and chuckles.

Sarah rolled her eyes and shook her head.

"Because of Sarah and Whiskey's contribution to solving mysteries and helping make Cottageville safer, I am hereby naming her Citizen of the Year and giving her the key to the city. Nobody deserves it more this year." Trish placed a six-inch brass key on a red silk string in Sarah's gloved hand and they paused in its transfer so photos could be taken for the official records and by *The Cottageville Courier* photographer. Afterward, Trish's assistant handed Sarah a framed Citizen of the Year certificate, and then Mayor Trish asked for an official round of applause for Sarah and Whiskey. Tears filled Sarah's eyes as she looked at the crowd. She felt so blessed to be a part of the community her grandmother had loved so much. She wished Gigi could have witnessed this day.

As Sarah made her way off the stage with Whiskey by her side, the mayor talked about the history of the town's big white pine tree and then she plugged in the colored lights as the high school's band launched into "Santa Claus is Coming to Town." Toward the end of the song, the fire department's ladder truck drove near the stage with Santa hanging from the back of it. It stopped. Santa stepped down, and dozens of small children screamed his name as he climbed the steps to the stage and then sat on the throne.

Mayor Trish explained that Santa would be available for photos and wish lists until seven tonight and then tomorrow and Sunday from eleven to three before he needed to return to the North Pole and finish the toys to be delivered Christmas Eve.

Sarah leaned down to Jared's ear and asked, "Do you need to sit on Santa's lap, big boy?"

"All of my Christmas wishes have already come true." He locked eyes with her and her heart fluttered like the first snowflake falling on a winter night—unexpected, beautiful, and impossible to ignore. She placed a sweet, soft, and swift kiss on his lips since they were in public.

As toddlers and preschoolers and their parents queued for Santa, Sarah pushed Jared to her booth. Ginger was mid-sale of an order of chicken dog biscuits and half a dozen candy cane and dark chocolate chunk scones, and Emily was fitting a sunflower yellow fleece jacket on Kahlo while Cassatt awaited her turn. Bill hugged and congratulated

Sarah, followed by Gladys and Mrs. Jenkins. When Ginger finished the transaction, she released a small squeal, handed Sarah a bouquet of yellow roses—her favorite—and hugged her bestie, followed by a hug for Jared. "Good to see you out and about, J. How are you feeling? And don't tell me like you were hit by a truck." She raised her eyebrows at him. "I'm onto you, mister."

Jared chuckled. "You know me too well, G. I'm good, especially since Sarah decided not to make a liar out of you when you were at the ER."

Ginger let out an astonished laugh, her cheeks flushing as she tried to cover up just how thrilled she was. "It's about freaking time," she mumbled.

"We're slow daters," Jared said.

"Glacial."

"Timing is everything. Speaking of which, do you think I can log part-time on the Java and Juice clock this week? I think if I sit on a high stool, I can work the register for at least the morning rush and you and Taylor can fill the orders."

Ginger gave a soft, under her breath chuckle, like she was experiencing a moment of private amusement. But Jared broke into it. "You didn't bet on it."

"No we didn't. We were in unison that you'd try to come back ASAP."

"Sitting around sucks." Half of Jared's mouth curled into a smile, like he was trying to hold back his amusement but couldn't quite keep it contained, a hint of mischief dancing in his eyes.

"I'm with ya. If you're up to it, let's start with three hours on

Monday and see how you do and feel. Six-thirty?"

"Oooo, I get to sleep in. Sounds good. Thanks, boss." Their usual start time was four a.m. to prepare and bake the day's specials and build the salads before they opened their doors at seven.

Ginger bent down and hugged him. "I'm just so glad you're still alive." When she pulled back, unshed tears glistened in her eyes.

"You and me both."

Ginger, Jared, Emily, Whiskey, and Sarah stayed at the booth helping customers, talking and joking around, and drinking hot chocolate until the Winter Wonderland wound down for the night at eight. Then Jared insisted Sarah load three boxes onto his lap to consolidate two trips to the car into one. Sarah and Emily agreed to reconvene when the festivities began at ten Saturday morning. Sarah promised to cover Ginger's part of the booth while Emily focused on the Coiffure's side until the Java and Juice cafe closed at two. And with that, they said goodnight.

Five minutes later, Sarah pulled into her driveway, thankful she remembered to leave on an inside light as it made her house look more inviting in the darkness. They had sold a number of festive outfits, leashes, and collars, as well as booked three grooming appointments and one nail clipping for next week, even though they were working a truncated week by taking Monday and Tuesday off to recover from working the weekend festival. She hoped the next two days at her Winter Wonderland booth she and Em would be just as busy as they were tonight.

Robert Wise had dropped by their booth to congratulate Sarah on being named Citizen of the Year, and to thank her and Emily again for taking such good care of "his boy". Poodle rescuers Daisy and Donovan, who Sarah and Gladys had helped in an emergency during the summer, came by to tell her how much they thought she deserved the award and they got a four-for-one visit because they arrived as Em was sizing jackets on Kahlo and Cassatt. They were thrilled to see their "former foster kids," as they called them. Kahlo seemed to recognize them as she gave one sharp yip, and with her tail beating staccato, wiggled toward them from atop the table where Gladys was trying to attach the Velcro straps under her belly. Daisy laughed and reached to scratch the dog under the chin.

Sarah smiled to herself as she recalled the evening and unlocked her front door with both Whiskey and Jared by her side. Her life felt full and rich and brimming with peace and contentment.

CHAPTER TWELVE

But all of that changed on Wednesday after the mailman delivered a stack of cards to Carter's Canine Coiffure. The business had been hopping all morning with clients whose humans wanted them to look and smell their best for the holidays. Emily and Sarah had each washed, blown dry, and clipped the nails of three dogs. Hank popped in and left six holiday cards, the electric bill, and the water bill on the counter. "Thanks, Hank," Sarah called, as she set Sprinkles the shih-tzu on the ground as Hannah Beau, Cottageville's Fire Chief, was due to pick her up in five minutes.

Whiskey sniffed Sprinkles, who took off toward the door, like she wanted to follow Hank to freedom. "Whoa there," Sarah raced after the twelve-pound black and white beast and scooped Sprinkles into her arms.

Once the door was firmly closed, she put Sprinkles back on the floor and opened the first card. The front had a red foil frame around an old-timey image of an Irish setter with a green bow around its neck. "Aww," Sarah said to herself admiring the dog. She opened the card to see who it was from and a folded eight and a half by eleven inch paper fell out, which she assumed was a Christmas letter.

She unfolded the white paper and said, "Oh my God! Oh my God!" Whiskey sped to her side and sat on Sarah's foot, like he wanted to provide comfort and grounding.

"What?" Emily asked, coming out of the bathroom in the back and wiping her hands on her apron.

Sarah had dropped the sheet of paper like it was a scorpion. Her eyes were wide open and unblinking. She fumbled with her back pocket trying to retrieve her phone. On the counter in front of her on that piece of paper were cut out letters from a magazine or newspaper. They spelled: COY? I'M COMING FOR YOU. A skull and crossbones had been drawn in a black Sharpie underneath the words.

Emily approached from the other side of the counter and reached out her hand to pick up the paper.

"Don't touch it," Sarah snapped. "Fingerprints."

Emily retracted her hand as if she had been bitten by a cobra. She leaned over the counter without touching anything. "Coy? I'm confused."

"I believe it's an acronym. Citizen of the Year." Sarah located the chief in her contacts and pressed the phone icon.

"Who would threaten you? It doesn't make sense. We all love you."

"Well, clearly someone doesn't." Into the phone Sarah said, "Chief James, something arrived in my mail today that you're going to want to see."

There was a beat while Sarah listened, then she said, "It's a note on folded paper inside a Christmas card and the words on the note are spelled with cut-out letters. Underneath is a skull and crossbones, hand drawn."

Silence again. Then Sarah said, "I'm the only one who has touched it. We will leave it where it is until you get here. Okay. See you in five." She disconnected and looked at Emily, who anxiety emanated from like heat radiating from a fire, intense and impossible to ignore.

"He's on his—" Sarah started at the same time Emily said, "Coming for you to what? Hurt you? Kidnap you? Challenge you? Kill you? I don't like this one bit. And who sends a threat inside a holiday card? Where's the good cheer in that?"

"I think that's the point," Sarah said, wiping her now-sweating hands on her apron. "Whoever sent it was going for the shock factor. They wanted me to be surprised."

"I'm beyond surprised," Emily said. "I'm scared for you."

"That's what whoever sent this wants: me to be frightened and looking over my shoulder. Well, I'm not going to do that. Anyone who was serious about doing me harm wouldn't forewarn me. Think about it. They'd just come at me. But this—" She flipped her hand above the counter. "This is either from a coward or from someone who wants to try to control me through fear. And I'm not going there. I refuse."

"But...but what if they are just playing with you before they strike to kill or maim, like cats do with birds? I don't like it. I don't like it one bit, Sarah."

The front door of the Coiffure opened and the Fire Chief and Chief James, wearing his uniform and hat, walked in at the same time. Sprinkles ran to her human while Whiskey ran toward Chief James, who mindlessly bent and scratched his head. "Hi, Whisk," he said. "I ran into Hannah on the sidewalk."

Hannah Beau was coatless and wore a white turtleneck under a red Cottageville Fire sweatshirt, faded jeans, and insulated duck boots. She scooped up her dog and kissed her little black nose. "I hope you were a good girl," she said to Sprinkles.

"She always is," Sarah said.

Chief James was looking at the mail on Sarah's counter as Emily took the money from Hannah and bid her a good day. Sprinkles looked so cute with a green and red bow around her collar and she seemed happy to be done with the grooming.

Chief James handled everything with gloves as he flipped through each card and checked their postmarks. He asked Sarah to open the still sealed cards to ensure there were no other threatening notes in the pile. Sarah set the two bills aside. The rest of the cards were holiday wishes from their clients and friends. Some of the stress Sarah had been holding for the last ten minutes lessened as she read the congratulatory messages on being named Citizen of the Year and missives of love. Her heart felt buoyed ... until the Chief pointed out that the threat had a Cottageville postmark. Okay, so someone in town had it in for her. Hmm. She guessed that made sense as it had to be someone who was at the Winter Wonderland or who read *The Cottageville Courier.*

"Has anyone handled this envelope, card, and paper besides you?"

"No. I wouldn't let Em touch it. But Hank delivered the mail so maybe he or someone at the post office did."

"All postal employees' prints are on file. And I believe we have yours and Em's too. Let's hope we get lucky and are able to pull a print and it's in the system." He put the card, paper, and the envelope, which was addressed to "Sarah Carter," with the Coiffure's full name and address stacked underneath in that same black marker, into an evidence bag. "In the meantime, don't go anywhere without Whiskey or at least one other person and be aware of your surroundings at all times. We have to take this seriously, even if it is someone's idea of a sick joke." The chief's mouth was set in a grim line, his gaze hard and unwavering, leaving no room for doubt about the gravity of his words.

Emily audibly sucked in a breath. "A joke? This can't possibly be a joke." But then her mouth clamped shut and her eyes grew like a cartoon character's when she realized the implication of the threat not being a joke. She gasped.

"Both of you," Chief James said, "call us immediately if you hear or see anything suspicious or if another one of these arrives." He held up the evidence bag. "Sarah, I'll be in touch soon. Please keep yourself safe."

At the chief's final statement, Whiskey let loose a whine of agreement. "That's right, Whiskey. Do your job and protect her." He scratched the red heeler's head again before leaving the Coiffure.

When the door was shut, Emily said, "I think I've lost my appetite for lunch. Who would want to harm you, Sarah? And why? You've never hurt anyone."

Sarah opened the counter and walked through, with Whiskey at her heels. "Not intentionally I wouldn't. But do you think it's a threat to me personally or do you think since it was addressed to me at the Coiffure and the note was in a dog card that it could be a threat to my business?"

Emily tilted her head just like Whiskey did sometimes. "You mean like 'coming for you' as in competition?"

"I'll admit that wasn't my initial reaction. But the more I think about it, it could be Moe's way of saying he's trying to take my customers." Sarah pulled her salad from the back fridge. "You sure you don't want lunch?"

"I'll eat with you. Especially now that you've brought up the fact that maybe it isn't as scary." Emily reached to take her salad from Sarah. They sat across from each other at a back table. Emily said, "Do you really think that's it?"

Sarah's ginger ponytail bounced as she shook her head. "I have no idea. I'm just trying to wrap my head around everything 'I'm coming for you' could mean." Sarah considered her talk in the park with John Beams. The police still hadn't released a public statement about the attack on Fiona. Had she received a written threat before being beaned on the skull?

When Sarah finished her salad, she went into the bathroom to brush her teeth and to avoid Emily inadvertently seeing her text to Officer Beams. "Chief may have told you I received something that could be a threat. Do you know if Fiona got one before she was attacked?"

She applied Chapstick to her lips while she waited for his three dots to turn into a text. "Don't know. She's still not conscious. We didn't see one when we searched. But we weren't looking for one either."

"Okay. Thanks."

"Be safe, Sarah."

Sarah tried to push the whole scenario to the back of her mind as she hung the holiday cards they had received over the past couple of days around the window frame. They had three more clients to service that afternoon, and they would take a lot of time and energy with their thick, multiple layer coats and size: Annabelle the sable akita, Max the malamute, and Homer the husky, who had just moved to town and was having his first visit to the Coiffure.

Homer was the first to arrive and he greeted Whiskey in husky-speak with a "rararara" and a thump of his front paws on the ground as he dipped his body. Whiskey responded with a "yip" and then flashed Homer and his human a big grin. Homer lived with Dennis Denali, a recently retired silver haired national forest ranger, who had always wanted a dog but couldn't because of the restrictions in the parks where he lived in federal housing. The day after he retired, he rescued Homer and moved to Cottageville, to be closer to his daughter and two preschool-aged grandchildren.

Sarah introduced herself to Dennis with a handshake while Emily took the dog's leather leash and led him into the grooming area. Whiskey kept pace with his new friend.

The Coiffure's front door opened just as Emily got Homer to

walk into a tub, and Annabelle pulled Drake Farmer through the front door. The way she was pulling made Sarah think she was serious about getting groomed...or maybe she was just excited at the prospect of seeing Whiskey, as he raced from his new friend to greet her and skidded to a stop right in front of her. She playfully nipped at his ear, and he smiled and stretched to press the side of his neck against hers.

Sarah took Annabelle from Drake and promised she'd be done in two hours. She gave the same time frame to Dennis, and then she and Emily got to work. Max was the last to arrive an hour and a half later, and Emily started him while Whiskey and Homer romped around the Coiffure and Annabelle was blown dry and brushed. Sarah tried to focus on the task in front of her, but after all of these years, grooming was second nature and gave her mind time to wander. And the more she dwelled on the possibilities of what the note could mean, the bigger the ball of angst in the pit of her stomach grew. Part of her wanted to demand the card sender show their face so at least she'd know who and what she was dealing with. But the other part of her was afraid she wouldn't like or survive the answer.

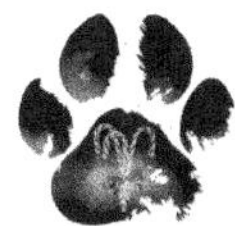

CHAPTER THIRTEEN

On Friday at five-thirty a.m. Sarah's alarm went off jarring her from a dream that featured her beloved Gigi. The dream started with Sarah at age five, learning how to make bread in her grandmother's kitchen, though that kitchen looked neutral toned like the current one in Sarah's house as opposed to the 1990's hunter green cabinets and ivy wallpaper border and white appliances Gigi had then. Sarah stood on a stool and learned to punch down the dough before its second rise. She loved its squishiness and slightly gummy texture and was awed by the way it seemed to breathe and expand over the course of an hour.

Afterward, they placed the bread in a preheated oven and as Sarah was watching through the glass door as it baked, her dream turned into a tie dye swirl of blues and greens and white and she found herself running as an adult through a forest, all alone, her heart pounding her chest, her mouth gulping for air, her legs not moving fast enough to escape what was pursuing her, something much bigger than herself that she felt but couldn't see. Just when she opened her mouth to scream, the ear-splitting beep, beep, beep woke her up.

She lay staring at the dark ceiling willing her heart rate to calm while Whiskey stood on her chest with his nose to hers. She whispered, "I'm okay, boy" though she wasn't sure she was.

"Sarah, are you okay in there? I thought I heard you scream." Jared said from behind her closed bedroom door.

"You can come in," she said. "I was having another bad dream."

He hobbled into her room on his crutches and stood at the foot of her bed. He wore an old Spiderman t-shirt with gray and black plaid flannel lounge pants. "Were you being chased again?"

Sarah released an audible breath. "Yep." Two nights in a row, Sarah had had similar dreams, and Jared was certain it had been triggered by the note. But he did agree with Sarah that they didn't have enough context to know if she was being physically or personally threatened, since it wasn't addressed to her at her home but instead to her business. But still, he was worried about the toll on her psyche and mental health the note was taking.

Jared maneuvered to the side of her bed. "Want for me to hug you or hold you?"

"Nah. I'll let the shower wash away the tension. But thanks." She scooted around him in her snowman sleep shirt and her dogs with candy canes flannel pj bottoms and went into her bathroom and shut the door.

Jared called after her, "I'll get your coffee ready."

"Thank you," she yelled through the closed door. "Can you let Whiskey out?"

"Sure thing. Come on, Whisk." Jared used his crutches to clomp after the dog to the back door.

Sarah stared into the mirror at her bloodshot eyes and the dark shadows beneath them, traces of sleepless nights and heavy thoughts etched onto her face like fading bruises. She couldn't stand it. She longed for joy and when her biggest worry was how she and Emily would get through Chutney's bath and nailing clipping without getting bit.

She loudly and intentionally exhaled trying to force the knot in her chest to move and unravel. She splashed cool water on her eyes and face in an attempt to relieve some of the puffiness. And then she turned on the shower and climbed into it and let tears of frustration fall.

Thirty minutes later, she and Whiskey strolled through the park, Whiskey with his nose to the ground sniffing the trails of raccoons, possums, and whatever else had passed through during the night. From a distance, Sarah spied a man sitting on the swing set. He wore a dark jacket and a Stetson. *Maurice*, she thought, before wondering what he was doing all alone in the park this morning. He didn't seem like a swing set kind of guy, more like someone who broke broncos.

Whiskey trotted right up to him and as Sarah followed, she noticed the trickle of tears down his cheeks and the hollowness of his gaze.

"Maurice," she said as she approached him. "It's me, Sarah. You sold me candy the night Fiona got hurt. Are you okay?" She stopped a few feet in front of him and at an angle to his swing. If he pushed off with his foot, she didn't want the moving swing to hit her.

Maurice reached down and stroked Whiskey's head and ears. When he looked up at Sarah, she saw his eyes were even more bloodshot than hers. "She's gone." His voice cracked. "Fiona. Didn't. Make. It." Each word was a struggle, as though speaking them aloud forced him to confront a reality he could barely accept, his shoulders slumping under the weight of the loss.

"I'm so sorry," Sarah said. "Would you like me to sit with you?"

Maurice shook his head no.

"Do you need anything?"

"Her. Alive," he whispered before burying his face in his hands.

Sarah didn't know what to do. Her instinct was to try to comfort him, but she barely knew him and since he didn't want her to sit with him, she wondered if she should leave him to his grief. She waited a few minutes while he cried and Whiskey sat near his boots waiting too or offering his head to scratch some more. But Maurice seemed to be lost inside his pain.

Eventually, Sarah patted his shoulder and said, "I'm around if you want to talk." He didn't respond or move his hands or head. With a final little squeeze of his shoulder, Sarah and Whiskey left Maurice alone in the quiet stillness of his sorrow.

When they returned to their house, Jared was dressed and waiting by the front door. Sarah relayed why she was a few minutes late as she drove him to Java and Juice. And for the first time, she broke her promise to John Beams and shared that Fiona had been hit on the head by an unknown assailant.

"So that means whoever attacked Fiona could be charged with murder," Jared said.

"Hmm, I'm not sure," Sarah said. "It might be manslaughter."

"What's the difference?" Jared asked just as they approached the cafe.

"I believe it is the intention behind it. I don't know if the police determined if the store was robbed and she was hit during the robbery or if she was attacked and that was the perpetrator's intention."

"Either way it is awful." Jared opened the passenger door and put the bottom of his crutches on the pavement before turning his legs toward the opening and dropping down from the Jeep.

"Agreed," Sarah said, waiting for Whiskey to jump over her seat and out of the vehicle.

Sarah held the door open for Jared and then she entered to get her second coffee of the day, breakfast, and hers and Emily's lunch salads, even though Java and Juice wasn't officially open for business. Whiskey was handed his chicken biscuit by Ginger herself, while Jared donned his apron and counted out the drawer in preparation to work. He was planning to sit on the stool at the register for a five-hour shift, the longest since his accident. But he was doing well, was pain-free, and liked being social with the customers as opposed to hanging out with only Whiskey to talk to at Sarah's. Taylor was refilling the refrigerated glass display cases with the freshly made pastries and daily specials. He had greeted both Sarah and Whiskey when they had entered and said "Hey" to Jared.

Ginger tilted her head at Sarah indicating she wanted to talk to her away from the counter so Sarah followed her to the furthest corner of the cafe, where Ginger adjusted the ceramic gingerbread men salt and pepper shakers that served as the centerpieces at this time of year on the bigger tables. "How long is he staying with you?" Ginger asked, her voice barely above a whisper.

"I don't know. He can't drive until the cast comes off so for now it is easier."

Ginger nodded her head. "Plus, he's worried about you."

Sarah raised her eyebrows, asking without saying a word how she knew.

"Sarah, he cares about you so much. He asked me how he could help you." Ginger's blue eyes searched hers.

"I don't have the answer to that. I don't even know what is going on."

"Have you heard anything from the chief?"

"Nope. But I really wasn't expecting to. Local postmark. Went through the mail system so there's the possibility of many prints. Unless I get more or something happens..." Her voice trailed off and she frowned like she hated the thought of that. "There isn't much to be done."

Ginger put her hand on Sarah's forearm. "I'm here if you need anything. Anything at all. We all are."

"I appreciate that. Sometimes waiting to see if anything happens is hard. Even more stressful than when you know something is coming and what it is."

"I can imagine. I have wine, a plethora of Christmas movies on streaming, and a basket full of facial, mani-pedi, and pampering products if you need a distraction. Whiskey and Jared are welcome, too."

Sarah chuckled. "That's sweet. Maybe on Sunday. Today, I need to do some online Christmas shopping before the Coiffure opens to ensure things get to my brother's place in time."

"May you find everything you need and at a good price," Ginger said, making her way back behind the counter. To Jared she said, "For our holiday specials, we have two special hot chocolates today: one with ginger and one with peppermint. We have nutmeg and pecan brittle scones, white chocolate and cherry filled eclairs, and candy cane sprinkled donuts filled with an eggnog creme anglaise."

Sarah's stomach growled in approval at the choices as she and Whiskey exited the cafe. They drove a few blocks to their business and locked themselves inside. Their first dog of the day wasn't due for an hour, so Sarah used that time to fold the towels that were in the dryer, to refill bottles and to tidy each station, and to select a luxurious sky blue cashmere sweater for her mother, a charcoal half-zip aran wool sweater for her dad, and an army green wool aran crewneck sweater for her brother. Since everything she ordered was made in Scotland, it was easy to have it delivered to her brother's Edinburgh address. Just before she pushed submit on the order, Sarah wondered if Jared might like a sweater, too. Or would he consider the cable knit, though well made, a bit mundane for his taste, which ran to plaids, henleys, and flannels in the fall and winter with jeans and comic book or super hero themed t-shirts in the summer. *He should probably have at least one well-made sweater,* she thought, *just in case he didn't already.* She closed out the order to be shipped to Scotland before placing a second order to be shipped to Cottageville. In that order she bought a green alpaca and merino blend scarf and a lightweight charcoal aran wool sweater for Jared plus a harris tweed blackwatch baker boy cap in a blue and green tartan for Ginger.

Sarah was closing her browser when her phone rang. "Good morning, Officer Beams," she answered.

"Good morning to you, Sarah. I hope I'm not interrupting."

"Not at all. What's up?"

"I'm calling to let you know that Fiona died early this morning. She never regained consciousness."

"That's so sad. I saw Maurice in the park early this morning. He was sitting on the swings and sobbing."

"We are calling it a homicide." Officer Beams cleared his throat.

Sarah hesitated before asking what she wanted to know. "Do you think it was manslaughter or murder?"

"We aren't sure. The only thing we do know is there was no sign of forced entry and the register looked undisturbed."

"So, she may have been targeted."

"Yes. Look, this is confidential—well, all of it is—but we found a civil protective order against a guy."

"A restraining order? Against Maurice?" Sarah reopened her computer.

"No. We're following up to see where that guy is."

"Um, okay. That makes sense. What was Fiona's last name again?"

"Fiore."

"So, you think whatever happened wherever they were before they came to Cottageville may have followed her or her and Maurice?"

"It's possible. But that doesn't mean you should let your guard down. Keep your doors locked when you and Em and Whiskey aren't all in there together."

"The doors are locked right now and I will continue to keep them that way." Just then a key turned in the front lock and Whiskey ran to the door with his tail wagging. "I've gotta go. Emily is here."

"Okay, Sarah. Be safe."

"You too, John. Thank you for calling." Sarah disconnected and greeted her assistant, who was sporting two extension braids today with red and green ribbons under a black velvet fisherman's cap. Sarah handed Emily a pastry and then let her know that Fiona never regained consciousness and had passed.

CHAPTER FOURTEEN

The Coiffure door seemed to be revolving with a stream of people and pets all morning. A number of people commented on Jared's vibrant painting of Whiskey. Sarah was thrilled with how well it turned out despite Jared's injuries, though they didn't seem to inhibit his ability to hold a brush.

Grooming appointments, nail clippings, two emergency situations, and a slew of shoppers following up on merchandise they had seen at Winter Wonderland and had decided to purchase. Dog sweaters and Hanukkah-, Kwanzaa-, and Christmas-themed collars plus an assortment of leashes and harnesses, brushes, and toys were snatched up by shoppers determined to be done with their holiday shopping as soon as possible. Sarah was grateful she and Emily took the time to install a wooden four-way spinning rack in the waiting area to hold the festival's overflow merchandise. At the rate things were walking out the door, Sarah was certain they'd have no backstock for next year's festival—and for that she was grateful. She hated to have to remember where she stashed things from one year to the next.

A few minutes after eleven, Sarah zipped out of the Coiffure and drove her vehicle to Java and Juice to pick up Jared and take him to her house. She left Whiskey with Emily, following Officer Beams' instructions about being cautious, even though the roundtrip took ten minutes and Emily had been working on a great Dane who would have also provided a line of defense.

It was late afternoon and Emily and Sarah both had wet and sudsy dogs in their tubs when the bells on the door jingled Hank's entrance. "Good day to you, Sarah and Emily," he said, placing the mail on the counter, before he bent to scratch both sides of Whiskey's neck. "You are looking good today, Whiskey. Have you recently been brushed?"

In answer, Whiskey flashed his black gums and white teeth at Hank.

"He was this morning," Sarah said. "Thanks for the mail, Hank. We'll see you again tomorrow." Since it was the holiday season, Sarah had extended the Coiffure's hours to include a half-day on Saturdays in order to fit in every pet. The rest of the year, she and Emily used Saturdays and Sundays as their days of rest.

Sarah pulled the bichon frisé from the tub in front of her and placed her on the table. French Fry's human was a nine-year-old boy who insisted his dog's head should look like a cotton ball so Sarah blew and styled and trimmed the white fur into a poof. Sarah felt a bit bad for the dog because she thought the cut made the bitch comical. *But then again, how could anyone take a dog named French Fry very seriously anyway,* she thought. *At least Bobby Davis was a sweet kid who knew how to care for his canine companion.*

After tying a red satin bow to French Fry's collar, Sarah put her on the floor to play romp with Whiskey. She asked Emily if she needed any help with a long-haired dachshund and when she said she didn't, Sarah moved on to opening the mail: four dog themed holiday cards from clients, a special offer for a new credit card that the Coiffure didn't need, a catalog from company that sold pet supplements and supplies, and an invitation to a holiday hoedown at Daisy and Donovan's. The hoedown looked like it would be fun and she wondered if Gladys got an invite too. She made a mental note to ask her.

The last thing Sarah opened was a legal size envelope with no return address. NAUGHTY SARAH CARTER and the Coiffure's address was written in black Sharpie on the front of the envelope, and it had a single light green elf stamp canceled with a Cottageville postmark. Sarah thought she recognized the block text. Before she opened the envelope, Sarah donned light latex gloves, just in case. Her heart thumped in her chest as she slit the top of the envelope with a knife.

A tri-fold white piece of computer paper was within, with cut-out letters pasted to one side: STILL COMING FOR YOU. WATCH YOUR BACK, FRONT, AND SIDES. Underneath those cut-out letters, the sender hand wrote in black, "He knows if you've been naughty or nice" along with a drawing of what could be a sack of coal.

Sarah gasped. She pulled her phone from her apron pocket and called the chief. When he answered she said, "Got another one. Please come."

Emily paused with the dachshund's right front paw in her hand. "You okay, Sarah?"

"Much as I can be. Got another threat. Chief James is on his way."

Sarah felt adrenaline coursing through her body and her hands started to shake. She angled her phone camera to capture the message on the paper without any overhead light glare. She took a photo of the envelope, too. She wished she had done that the first time so she could have shown Jared the actual message. But she hadn't thought of it.

Whiskey and French Fry ran to the front door as it opened and the chief stepped inside followed by a blast of cool air. "Whiskey, who is your cotton candy friend?" He chortled to himself.

Sarah used her gloved finger to shove the letter and envelope to the chief's side of the counter. His eyes skimmed the message before he said, "I'm sorry, Sarah. We will get to the bottom of this."

Sarah glared at the paper like it was a viper ready to strike. "You don't think it's related to what happened to Fiona, do you? Did she receive any threatening messages?"

"We didn't see any in the trash or her files when we searched the place."

"Is anyone else who operates a business in Cottageville receiving threats?"

"Not that we know of." Chief James searched Sarah's face. "I know it is unsettling, Sarah. You don't have any old scorned loves, or does Jared? I heard you are a couple now and he's living with you."

Sarah's eyes widened. "No, no old boyfriends. No idea about Jared. And we aren't living together. I mean, yes, he has been living at my house since his accident, but we aren't living together living together, if you know what I mean."

"And you don't owe anyone money, right?"

"What? No. Absolutely not. I live debt-free."

"That's good," Chief James said. "I know before we weren't sure if it was a general threat to your business or to you personally. But this naughty comment makes me think it is more personal." The chief lowered his voice and asked, "Are you into kink or BDSM or anything?"

Sarah felt her eyes practically pop from her head in amazement at his question, her gaze widening as though trying to grasp his possible thoughts about her and the words hanging between them. "What? No. Not at all. Is there even a place for that here? I mean, no. I wouldn't even. Not that there's anything wrong with—."

Chief James cut her off. "It's okay, Sarah. I just had to ask. Calm down. The sender called you 'naughty' so I'm trying to understand why or how that label fits."

"It doesn't." Sarah was emphatic like a judge issuing a sentence.

Chief James put the envelope and paper into an evidence bag. "We'll run it for prints again. The last one had postal employees and yours. So I'm not expecting much from this. Please don't go anywhere alone or without Whiskey and keep your doors locked when you can. Call me if you get anything else or see anything suspicious. We'll get to the bottom of this, Sarah. I promise you."

"You'd better," she said barely above a whisper. "I don't want to end up like Fiona."

The chief reached a hand toward Sarah's gloved hand and he squeezed. "I don't want that either, and besides, I don't think the two things are connected."

"But you don't know. There's so much we don't know about this or what happened to her." She squeezed his hand back and searched his eyes, trying to unearth any secrets he might know.

"That's true. And we have to stay open to any possibility right now. I'll have my officers swing by here during business hours and past your house after hours. We'll figure this out, Sarah. We will." He gave her hand one final squeeze before Whiskey and French Fry escorted him to the door.

Sarah started a three-way text with Jared and Ginger. "G—can you and Daniel come for dinner tonight? I need my peeps. Got another letter."

Jared responded first. "Are you okay?"

"Maintaining," Sarah wrote in response.

Ginger wrote, "OMG. I'll let Daniel know. 6? What can we bring?"

"Wine," Jared responded. "I'll make the rest. Sarah, just us four?"

"Yes. And 6 is good." Sarah believed four brains were better than one. Maybe if they brainstormed, they could determine who was messaging her and why and figure out a way to stop it.

An hour and a half later Sarah and Emily cleaned the Coiffure and prepped for the next day. The front door was locked and Whiskey had stretched out against it, waiting for them to finish the chores. As Sarah swept the floor for one last time today, she acknowledged to herself how drained she felt. The nightmare and emotional highs and lows of the day had exhausted her as if she were a greyhound who spent too much time and energy running around a track. She wanted to be like Whiskey and curl into a ball and take a nap.

Jared had checked with her that salad and lasagna was okay for the meal. She told him she'd see if the candy store was open and would buy chocolate for dessert if it was. He gave that a texted thumbs up. When they removed their aprons and were saying goodnight, Sarah asked Emily if she wanted to walk with her to the pop-up shop.

Emily shivered before saying, "Yes. I'll go. Let's just not find someone in a medical emergency this time."

"Agreed."

Whiskey walked with them the short way there, and then Sarah turned and said, "You probably need to stay out here, Whisk. We'll only be a minute. Sit and be a good boy." He parked his furry butt on the sidewalk and watched through the glass floor to ceiling windows as they went inside.

Wearing his ever-present Stetson, steel toed work boots, Wranglers, and a gray and black flannel shirt, Maurice stood at the register with his face devoid of emotion, his eyes shifting around the room but watching no one. A handful of customers—all women wearing knit hats and coats except for one man in work boots, a quilted wool plaid shirt, and jeans—were plucking goodies from the baskets. The man stood apart, as he was not with the women who were clearly friends. He side-eyed each of the women, including looking Sarah and

Emily up and down, instead of paying attention to the candy he seemed to select at random and add to his bag.

"Hello, ladies." Maurice greeted Sarah and Emily.

"Hi, Maurice," Sarah said. She wanted to mention again how sorry she was for his loss, but she didn't want to draw attention to him in front of the other customers, all of whom she didn't know.

She and Emily busied themselves picking out milk and dark chocolates molded into holiday shapes: wreaths, reindeer, Santas, stockings, trees, candles, and ornaments. Sarah skipped the naughty elves this time, not feeling too friendly towards that word. She picked out enough chocolate for a party of twelve and took them to the register.

"Did you find everything you needed?" Maurice asked while he rang up her purchases.

"Yes, thank you." Sarah tried to catch his eye to gauge how he was doing.

He kept his eyes fixed downward, told her the total, ran her card, and thanked her for the purchase—acting like he didn't know who she was or that they had talked in the early morning. "Next," he said to Emily, and went through the same routine with downcast eyes, as if he really didn't want them to acknowledge anything that had happened.

Sarah took that as her cue and kept her mouth shut as she left the store and reconnected with Whiskey.

"Weird," Emily said. "I swear he was transmitting 'don't ask anything, don't say anything,' over and over again to us."

"He was indeed. I'd really like to ask him about threatening letters, but it was clearly not the time or the place."

When they got back to the Coiffure, Emily said, "Sarah, why

don't I drive you home? I know Whiskey is with you and people are out and about, but Chief James doesn't want you by yourself. So let me take you home."

"Do you want to stay for dinner? I'm sure we have plenty. Jared made lasagna and salad, and Ginger and Daniel are coming over." Sarah let Whiskey into the back seat of Emily's Honda before sliding into the passenger seat.

"Nah. You guys have your double date. Taylor's taking me for a burger. And tomorrow night Travis is taking me out for sushi." She grinned. "Life is good."

"Sure sounds like it is." Sarah's smile was so big it squinched up her eyes. "Sure there's not a third guy in the wings? Sounds like you have Sunday free."

"Ha ha," Emily said. "Sundays are me-time."

"Good for you." While she was enjoying Jared's company, Sarah realized it had been a while since she had some time to herself. But of course, if the threats continued, her friends wouldn't leave her alone for a moment so me-time would be a long time coming.

CHAPTER FIFTEEN

The evening started off great. Jared met her at the door with a friendly kiss and a hug, his warmth instantly putting her at ease. The aromas of tomato sauce and melting cheese drifted through the air, tantalizing her taste buds and hinting at the comfort food he'd prepared. Sarah felt herself relax, already knowing this would be a night to savor with her closest of friends.

"Need any help?" Sarah asked, placing the bag of chocolates on the granite counter.

"I have everything under control, mi'lady." Jared dipped in a bow as much as the crutches under his armpits would allow.

"Good. Then I'm going to take a shower and find some clothes that are not covered in pet hair and dander."

Jared flashed her a lopsided grin that highlighted one of his dimples, a playful glint in his eyes that made her heart skip, drawing her in without him even trying. She pressed her lips quickly to his before leaving the room.

"I'll have wine ready for you when you're done. I've decanted a spicy zin," he called after her.

"Sounds delicious." Sarah shut the door of her bedroom, sat on the end of her bed, and closed her eyes for a few minutes. She focused on her breathing, inhaling to a count of five, holding the breath for five, and exhaling for five before repeating the sequence three times. The tension in her neck and jawline started to ease. She sat with her feelings for Jared and let the warmth spread through her chest. She couldn't let herself get caught up in the letters. There had to be an explanation.

Sarah stripped off her clothes and put them in the basket in her walk-in closet. She turned the water on hot and stepped into the shower, letting the cascade wash away her worries. Tonight, she'd let herself be buoyed by those she loved best.

Sarah emerged from her bedroom ten minutes later with her hair still wet from its shampoo. She wore a navy *Feliz Navidog* Nordic-style sweater featuring a replicated image of Whiskey and his name emblazoned under his picture paired with navy yoga tights and sheepskin lined suede bootie slippers.

"You looked adorable. And what a great rendering of Whisk." Jared handed her a light pour of red wine. "Let me know what you think of this."

She took a sip. "Ooo, forward fruit, peppery finish. I like it."

"I do, too."

Whiskey batted Sarah's leg with his paw.

"Aww, do you want something, too? How about dinner?"

"Ruuuffff." He tapped his empty bowl with his paw, as if to say, "Get a move on it."

Sarah rolled her eyes. "You're too much, dog." She picked up his bowl, emptied a packet of his raw food into it, and then placed it back on his bone-shaped mat. "Are you sure you don't need help with anything?" she asked Jared before taking another sip of the wine.

"You could set the table. Carrying around a stack of plates is challenging."

"Of course." Sarah pulled four salad plates and four dinner plates from the shelving and added forks, knives, and spoons to that, as well as four red cloth napkins to add a festive touch. She carried those to her dining table. She went back into the kitchen to get water glasses and filled a clear glass pitcher from the tap and added those to the table.

Her front door knob jiggled with someone trying to open it, and Whiskey barked as he raced to confront the intruder.

"I'm coming," Sarah yelled over the din. "Whiskey, sit," she said when she got to the door. She unlocked the deadbolt and opened the door.

"I was just about to pull out my key," Ginger said. Her hair was in braids that hung on each side of her face under a blue knit cap that enhanced the hue of her eyes. Daniel stood behind her holding a bottle of wine in one hand and a box of what Sarah guessed were pastries in his other. He wore a puffy vest over a wool shirt, dark jeans, and tennis shoes.

"Beams and the chief told me to keep everything locked so I was following their orders."

"Understandable," Ginger said. "We don't want anyone to be able to get to you either." She gave Sarah a hug and then pulled a treat out of her coat pocket for Whiskey, while Sarah hugged Daniel.

They added their coats to the wooden tree rack in Sarah's entryway, and Ginger removed her boots and placed black ballet-style slippers that she had pulled from her back pocket on her feet. She padded into the kitchen while saying, "Something smells delicious. It's like a trattoria in here."

"Wine?" Jared asked his boss and Daniel, while holding up the bottle of zinfandel for their inspection.

"Yes, please," Ginger said.

"Sounds good." Daniel read the back of the bottle. "Napa, huh?"

"I didn't even look to be honest," Jared admitted. "The art on the bottle was the draw." He chuckled and shrugged his shoulders.

"It is cool," Daniel said. "Sounds similar to how I'd choose a wine. I know more about beer...or whiskey."

At his name, the dog's ears periscoped and turned to hone in on the source, ready for whatever he might be offered.

"Sorry, buddy." Daniel squatted down on the kitchen floor to where Whiskey was lying in the middle of the action. He ran his hand from the dog's head to the middle of his back over and over. Whiskey sighed and relaxed into the attention.

"Dinner will be ready in about ten minutes," Jared said. "Sarah, can you please get the salad out of the fridge and take it to the table?"

Daniel stood again and saw Jared leaning and balancing on one foot, trying to maneuver the heavy stoneware lasagna pan from the oven. "Hey, Jared, why don't you let me handle that?"

Jared glanced over his shoulder at Daniel and said, "Yeah. Thanks." He handed Daniel the potholders and hopped out of the way.

Daniel pulled out the layers of noodles, meat, sauce, and cheese while declaring, "Wow. This must weigh seven or eight pounds. Are you ready for this to go to the table and is there a trivet?"

"Umm, yep. It's ready. It has a lot of layers." Jared popped the tray of bread with garlic spread and a sprinkle of parmesan into the oven and turned it to broil. He left the oven door cracked open and peeked through the opening to ensure he grabbed the tray before the tops of bread burnt.

Sarah's voice came from the dining area. "Daniel, I have the trivet."

After sitting down and filling their plates, Ginger raised her glass. "To friendship and to keeping Sarah safe."

"Thanks, guys," Sarah said.

"Speaking of which," Jared said, "I know your initial offer was for me to be here a few days and it's now been over a week. But I'd prefer to stay with you until we know who the letter sender is and why. I know I'm not much in the way of defense with my cast and crutches, but knowing you aren't alone and Whiskey and I are both here may be a deterrent. What do you say, Sarah? Can I stay until the police have figured this out?"

Sarah's eyes filled with unshed tears. "Yes. Thank you." She reached out and squeezed his hand—but not too hard as she didn't want to aggravate his cuts and bruises.

Ginger put a forkful of lasagna in her mouth and chewed, a moan of pleasure escaping her closed lips. "Oooo, you should totally make this for the cafe. We'd make a mint just on this dish. It is that good. Seriously, Jared. Let's talk about it. I'll pay you a percentage on top of your hours."

"Once I'm back on both feet."

Ginger nodded. "Okay. So, Sarah. Spill the details. What did the letter say this time? What did the police say?"

"Hon, maybe let her eat some food first," Daniel suggested, putting his hand on Ginger's arm that was closest to him.

"It's okay," Sarah said. She got up from her chair, walked into the kitchen, and came back with her phone, which she had left on the counter. She opened the photos app, selected the photo of the letter, and passed her phone to Ginger who considered it before passing it around the table.

"Son of a—" Ginger said, voice dying under the weight of her frown.

"I know." Sarah's tone was flat. "But here's the thing you may not know..." Sarah started as her phone made its way back to her, and she told Ginger and Daniel the story about finding Fiona, her swing set meeting with Officer Beams, and then learning of Fiona's death, a homicide. She ended with, "What I don't know is if these two things are somehow related or totally separate incidents?"

Ginger shivered as Sarah finished. Very calmly and quietly she said, "So you aren't sure if someone's coming for you the way they went for Fiona." It wasn't a question.

"No, it can't be," Daniel said at the same time Sarah said, "Exactly."

"Did she get threatening letters?" Jared asked, his brows almost knit together in worry.

"I don't know. Chief James said he didn't know of any and that they didn't find any inside the pop-up shop. Oh, and by the way, we're having chocolate from there for dessert."

"What about in the Dumpster?" Ginger asked. "Did they look there?"

"I have no idea," Sarah said. "It wasn't specifically mentioned." She sopped up some sauce with a hunk of garlic bread. *God, it was good. Ginger was right. This should be on Java and Juice's menu.*

"Well then let's go check." Ginger stood up like she wanted to go right this very minute.

"Um, babe, can you wait until we are done with dinner?" Daniel rubbed her lower back. "There is still food on our plates."

"Okay," Ginger collapsed back into her seat and started to shovel food into her mouth. It was clear to the other three that she was over savoring every bite. She was on a mission to be done.

"Sorry, Jared," Sarah mumbled before imitating her BFF.

Daniel eyed his partner before saying, "Ging, I don't think you or you and Sarah should check out the Dumpster yourselves."

"And why not?" Ginger challenged.

"Because it's filled with garbage and germs and rats probably and who knows what else?"

"I'm not afraid of those things." She folded her arms over her chest and stared at Daniel. "And do you know Sarah? She's going to do everything within her power to stop this, and I can't let her do that alone."

"Then let me go with you," Daniel said.

"No," Ginger said. "Jared shouldn't stay here alone. Stay with him. We've got this and we'll return soon."

"Maybe you should let the police handle it," Daniel suggested.

"Oh, please. They have enough to do in this town. It's one small Dumspter. It wouldn't take long for us to search it. And if we find anything, of course, we'll call Chief James."

Daniel said nothing else as he finished eating. He eyed Jared a few times, but it was clear to Sarah that Daniel knew how strong-willed his woman was and she was, and he was unhappily waving a white flag of defeat.

As soon as their plates were clean, Sarah carried them into the kitchen while Ginger issued orders to the guys. "Get online and find out everything you can about Fiona Fiore and her partner Maurice. Hey, Sarah, do you think the notes could be from him? Like that he's providing competition to the Coiffure with his mobile grooming?"

"I don't think so. I mean, I don't think his business has much traction. John said he's either been at the hospital with Fiona or managing the candy store since the day I found her in the back." She loaded the dishwasher and then let Whiskey out to do his business in the backyard. He peed quickly and raced back inside for a freeze-dried liver treat.

"I wonder if Luella or any of the other employees at the post office could help us with the letter. Like maybe one of the carriers picked it up from a residential mailbox and would recognize it," Daniel said. "I know when I accidentally put my credit card payment into the mail slot without stamping it first, she was willing to go through the pile to find it and return it to me."

"That's a good idea to ask her," Jared said. "One of the big differences from living here than in a city is we get more personal service since we know our neighbors."

"That's something to follow up on tomorrow," Ginger said. "Right now, Sarah and I are going Dumpster diving before the service comes tomorrow to empty everything in downtown. Bestie, do you have any old things I can wear that you don't care if they get smelly or torn?"

"I'm sure I've got something," Sarah said, heading toward her bedroom with Ginger trailing behind her.

"More wine?" Jared asked Daniel. "Looks like we may be eating chocolates alone while snooping around the web. My tablet and laptop are on the bed in there." Jared pointed to the spare bedroom. "Would you be so kind as to get them?"

"Sure thing. Mind if I make a pit stop in your bathroom?"

"Help yourself." Jared poured more wine for himself and for Daniel, and he opened the bag of chocolates while he waited.

Sarah and Ginger emerged from Sarah's bedroom in hoodies with the hoods drawn over their hair and tied under their chins. Sarah's was black and Ginger's was an inky green. They both had on old jeans whose knees were ripping through. Sarah wore black suede lug sole boots, while Ginger had on Sarah's black Wellies.

"Wish us luck," Ginger said, kissing Daniel on the lips as he walked toward the table with the electronics.

"I will, but for the record, I'm still not digging this idea."

"Noted, love of my life. We'll be careful. I promise." She kissed Daniel again.

Sarah leaned down and kissed Jared on the lips. "Ginger's driving us so we shouldn't be gone long."

"Okay. You may want to take black garbage bags," Jared said.

"Ooo, good thinking. We may find things to bring back and examine," Sarah said, shoving her phone into her back pocket.

"Yes, but also to sit on. If you are truly going inside that big garbage receptacle you don't want to get that gross stuff all over her car. And don't forget flashlights."

"Oh, good points." Sarah ran into the kitchen and pulled a bunch of bags from under the sink and tore them from the roll. Then she grabbed two flashlights from the front closet and checked to make sure the batteries were fresh enough for them to work.

As she was getting the batteries, Sarah heard Daniel ask Jared, "Are you okay with this, man?"

"Not thrilled. But let's face it, we've barely been a couple so I don't think I should have a say. And I certainly would never tell my boss what to do." He chuckled. "But I am expecting them to be careful."

Though her back was to them, Sarah smiled to herself.

"Love you both," Ginger said, before they left the house.

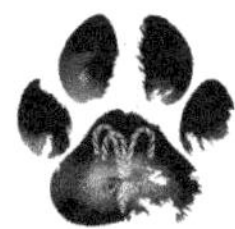

CHAPTER SIXTEEN

At nine on a Friday evening very few things were open in downtown Cottageville, where holiday wreaths adorned every black lamp post and the bulbs inside the lanterns cast a warm golden glow into the just above freezing temperature air. All of the stores were closed. The restaurants were wrapping up their supper service. The two bars on Main Street were the only places where people were milling about outside to smoke or to say their goodnights. On the north end of the street, the part closest to the park and to Sarah's house, sat Butch's Brewery, an old-timey drinking establishment with a biker bar vibe—with occasional fights and police raids for drugs—that had been bought and slightly rehabilitated into a brewpub by a guy in his thirties named Antonio "Butch" Cassava. Moe's Mobile Grooming van sat at the curb facing the door, which caused Sarah to assume Maurice might be inside the brewery. She hoped he wasn't drowning his sorrows too much. The second Main Street bar was further south, one block from the candy pop-up shop and two blocks from the Coiffure. It had labeled itself a lounge and featured live music on weekends. The bass reverberated from the building and its closed solid wood door, seeping into Ginger's car despite its rolled-up windows. No one was outside smoking or loitering and no one was walking on the sidewalk in this part of town.

They passed the candy store and as they did Sarah started counting the businesses to the end of the block. She wanted to be sure she could locate it from the back. Ginger drove to the end of the block and made a right and turned right again in the alley and parking areas that ran the length of Main Street.

The alley and paved blacktop for parking was deserted of people, but Sarah spied a raccoon waddling behind a garbage can seconds before the can's lid crashed to the pavement. "Geez," Ginger said. "They are so cute with their masks and creepy little hands and fluffy fur, but they are so destructive."

"Yes, they are," Sarah laughed. "Did you know in German they are called 'washing bears' since they use those 'creepy little hands,' as you called them, to wash their food before they eat it?"

"Nope. That's my something new I learned today. Where should I stop?"

"At this next one, I think. It should be the fifth from the end."

"I'm gonna leave the car running and its lights on. What do

you think?"

"Um, that's not exactly stealth mode."

"I know, but after seeing that raccoon, who knows what is in there. And it isn't like what we are doing is illegal."

"Are you sure about that?" Sarah hit the browser on her phone. "We probably should have Googled that before we left the house. Hey, Siri, can I get arrested for Dumpster diving in Iowa?"

The electronic voice said, "While Dumpster diving is not considered illegal in Iowa, local jurisdictions may have different ordinances and regulations especially when it comes to trespassing on private property."

"Good to know," Sarah mumbled.

"I'm sorry. I missed that. What did you say?" Siri asked.

Sarah put her phone on silent.

"You ready for this?" Ginger asked, getting out of the car. The headlights illuminated the large green metal rectangle in front of them.

"Umm, that's taller than the one behind the Coiffure. How do we get up? Maybe we should have brought a ladder."

"No need," Ginger said. "Put your hands like this or I will..." She clasped her fingers of both hands together into a cup at waist level. "And you can either boost me up or I'll boost you."

Sarah eyed the Dumpster and then her friend. "This seems like my battle. I'll go. You boost me."

"Sweetie, it's all of our battle. Someone fights one of us, they fight us all." Then she allowed Sarah to place her boot into her cupped hands to get leverage on the lip of the Dumpster. Sarah flipped her right leg over the lip and dangled there for a second before launching herself inside. She landed with a soft thud.

"You okay in there?" Ginger asked.

"Yep. It doesn't smell very good. Metallic and rotten something. Hang on. I'm turning on my light."

Sarah scanned the space with the flashlight beam. The sides of the rectangle had dribbles and chunks of something brown and thick. Sarah wasn't sure if it was some kind of used oil or molasses—though it smelled like neither. She started at the far end of the Dumpster and using her latex kitchen-gloved hands, she sorted through some scraps of newspaper and junk mail and empty cans of tuna—and she silently cursed people who didn't recycle. She moved aside what reeked like a plastic bag filled with used cat litter and bent to check out the formerly white papers that were crushed beneath it. Those papers were stained, wrinkled, and balled. She flattened them as best she could, but none of them had cut and pasted letters or any kind of threats. She searched through every inch of the Dumpster from its left side and both corners to its middle and couldn't find anything of importance.

Then Sarah waded to the other end of the receptacle and planned to work her way back to the middle. When she stepped into the right corner and placed her boot on what she hoped was the bottom of the can, she wobbled unsteadily. What she landed on wasn't the bottom and it wasn't flat. It felt through her boot sole like a rod of some kind. She kept her left boot planted on whatever it was and crouched down until her hands could feel around her foot. *What in the—?* She slid her hands around the perimeter of the item, recognizing it by its shape.

Sarah shoved the flashlight into the front pouch on her hoodie as she knew she'd need both hands for what she was trying to unearth.

She stood on the wooden handle of what felt like a sledgehammer. She backed her boot up a bit, grasped the handle, and lifted it. The thing had to weigh close to ten pounds. Organic matter, papers, discarded wrappers, and even some kind of liquid cascaded as Sarah brought it from the Dumpster floor. Once she had it up into the open, she held it in her left hand by the end of the handle. Then Sarah reached back into her pouch and pulled out the flashlight. The head of the mallet had a dark stain that provided a type of glue for the bits of hair and skin that had adhered to it.

Sarah felt her stomach heave and bile rise to the back of her throat. Her intuition screamed that this was the weapon that killed Fiona.

"Ginger," Sarah yelled. "Call the chief and tell him we need him or John or Candace immediately."

"You okay in there?"

"Yes. Just do it now."

"Okay. Calling."

Sarah listened as Ginger spoke into her phone. Her heart was racing and she wished she could get out of the can. But she knew she'd need to show the cops exactly where she found the sledgehammer. She wished she could set it down as it was a lot of weight to hold aloft. But she didn't want to contaminate the evidence any more than it already had been with all of the crap thrown on top of it.

Sarah trained the flashlight on the corner where she found the hammer to see if anything else jumped out at her. All of the surface trash looked recent.

"Sarah, Chief James said he's on his way. Beams is on patrol so he might get here first. What'd you find? More notes?"

"Nope. No notes. At least I didn't see any."

"So what'd you find?"

"You'll see soon enough."

Tires crunched gravel on the alley and came to a stop to the right of Ginger's Chevy Tahoe. Sarah heard a door open and then John Beams' voice greeted Ginger. "Do I even want to know what you're doing here?"

"Hi, John," Sarah yelled from inside the Dumpster. "It's a nice night for diving."

"Very funny." John opened the trunk of his cruiser and retrieved a rope ladder. He unraveled it and hooked it over the side of the Dumpster and stepped on the first rung.

"That would have been so much easier," Ginger said.

He rolled his eyes at her. "How'd she get in there?"

"I boosted her."

"Impressive." He climbed the rest of the way up the ladder until he could see inside. "Holy—."

"Exactly." Sarah cut him off. She held the sledgehammer by its twenty-inch handle and offered it to him after noticing he was wearing gloves.

"I'll be right back," he said to her. He climbed back down the ladder as Ginger said, "Oh my God. Is that—?"

"We won't know until we run the tests." Officer Beams was quick to say.

"Of course. But it sure looks suspicious."

Chief James' car squealed to a stop next to Beams' panda car and he hopped out. "I'll get the big bag from the trunk," he said, rifling for an appropriate size evidence bag.

John passed off the sledgehammer to him to bag. "I'm climbing in to find out from Sarah where she found it."

"I'll radio for the techs. It's gonna be a late night."

"Anything I can do to help?" Ginger asked.

"No," Chief James started to say but then said, "yes, actually. Call your man and ask him if Buck and Son sells Fiskar sledgehammers."

"Okay, I can do that. May I tell him why I am asking?"

Chief James looked up and down the alley and at all of the buildings around them, some apartments above the businesses and lights on. "Until you're in the privacy of your own home, just tell him one was found under suspicious circumstances."

"Gotcha."

Chief James used his car radio to bring in the crime scene techs. Ginger phoned Daniel, asked the chief's question, and said she wasn't sure when she and Sarah would make it back, but that she'd stay in touch. John Beams climbed back up the ladder and talked with Sarah, learning why she had climbed into the Dumpster in the first place and where she had found the hammer. She pointed, and as if he read her mind he said, "I know you'd love to keep sifting through the garbage, but it is time for you to come out. I'm declaring this an official crime scene and I'm pissed we neglected to go through it before."

Sarah felt bad for her friend. "In your defense, when I found her we didn't know someone had attacked her."

"Yes, but when we processed the store we should have processed the Dumpster, too. It was sloppy of us not to."

"Or," Sarah countered, "maybe the sledgehammer wasn't even here then. We don't know. It could have been ditched after she died."

"Maybe. But you did say it was near the bottom. Come on, Sarah, let me help you out of there." He reached out his hand to her. When she tried to gain traction with her lug soles on the Dumpster's walls, her foot slid and she would have fallen on her butt if not for John's iron grip on her wrist.

"Hang on a sec," he said, letting her wrist go, after making sure she was on solid footing. He disappeared from Sarah's view and suddenly the base of the rope ladder arced into the bin. "Climb up and when you get to the top, perch on the lip and flip the ladder to the outside."

"Okay." Sarah did as she was told. "So much easier," she said once her feet landed on the pavement. One glance at her legs told her Jared was right to have them bring black plastic for the car seats. Bits of food, splashes of liquid, and things Sarah didn't even want to identify clung to her jeans and the suede of her boots. "Disgusting."

"And you don't smell very good either," John said.

"You won't either after you get through tonight."

"That's for sure," he agreed.

Chief James joined them next to the Dumpster and in a couple of seconds so did Ginger. "Daniel said no Fiskars in his store. He said the big box home improvement stores usually carry that brand. His are almost all metal heads with fiberglass handles." She shrugged her shoulders. "I noticed that one's handle was wood."

"Very observant," Chief James said. "Did you get their statements and the location of the hammer?" he asked his officer.

"Unofficially, and yes, she pointed to where it was."

"Sarah, if I get a pad of paper from my car, will you draw a diagram for us?"

"Absolutely." She waited for the chief to emerge from his trunk with a legal pad and pen and then Sarah used the hood of Ginger's car as a desk while Ginger held the flashlight over her shoulder. In a few minutes, she had a rough outline with an X marking the approximate location. "The hammer was buried under about a foot, maybe a foot and a half of stuff so it was close to the floor, but I'm not sure if it was on the floor or if papers or something were under it. The bottom of the can felt a little rough in parts. I can't remember if it felt that way under the hammer. But to be honest, when I realized what was under me, my heart was beating so fast I thought it would explode. I registered the implication of finding a giant hammer behind the shop." A chill ran through Sarah.

"I understand," Chief James said. "Ginger, why don't you take her home and get her cleaned up. Sarah, we'll stop by tomorrow for an official statement and your signature."

Sarah was quiet on the short drive to her house. Main Street looked desolate, and where she once saw warmth and invitation in the glow of the lampposts, she now saw only shadows, drifting snowflakes, and a creeping sense of suspicion. *Who in Cottageville would commit such a brutal, wicked crime?* Tears lurked in her eyes, ready to ambush her the moment she let her guard down, threatening to spill over in the safety of the darkened car.

In the entryway of Sarah's house Whiskey's nose wiggled frantically up and down her boots and jeans like he couldn't understand the mixture of scents and what it could all mean. Jared wrapped his arms around her, not seeming to care how much she stank.

"I should probably take off these boots and jeans and everything else outside," Sarah said, turning to open the front door again.

"It's freezing out there and you'll flash the neighbors." Jared kissed her ear.

"Okay, I'll just strip here," Sarah said, bending over to untie her boots.

"Umm, I'm going to...um...go into Jared's bathroom and wait until the coast is clear," Daniel said.

Sarah chuckled. "Sorry about that, Daniel. I wasn't thinking about the effects of my undressing in the doorway."

Ginger laughed and said, "I left my clothes in your room, Sarah, and since I didn't dive into the Dumpster, I'm clean enough to walk through your house. I'll bring you a towel."

"Thanks." Sarah was down to her bra and panties when Ginger returned with the towel. Sarah wrapped it around herself and said, "Excuse me. Please let Daniel know he can come back out." Then she padded barefoot into her bathroom and shut the door.

CHAPTER SEVENTEEN

After her second shower of the day and now wearing paw print flannel pjs and her *Feliz Navidog* sweater again, Sarah found her three friends in the living room, eating chocolate, and drinking wine. Whiskey was lying on a big dog bed near the coffee table. He was on his back, his legs were up in the air, but his wrists were bent so his paws were drooped back toward his chest, and his neck was angled into a J. His snoring added a soundtrack to the quiet conversation. Ginger had told the men what they had found while Sarah was ridding herself of the stench and decay. She had moved her stinky boots back outside and put her clothing in the washer by itself so it wouldn't contaminate anything else she owned. She had considered just disposing of it all, but she hated to waste anything. And who knew when she'd need the clothes to Dumpster dive again, she giggled to herself.

As she curled up next to Jared on the sofa, he handed her a glass of wine with his left hand and put his right arm around her, pulling her closer.

"So what did you guys find?" Sarah asked.

"Restraining orders against three different men."

"What?" Sarah asked, not sure she heard him right.

"They go back years," Jared said.

Sarah's eyes narrowed for a second like her brain and heart hurt. "Any with her same last name?"

"None that we saw," Daniel said.

"So Fiona picked abusers?" Ginger's voice sounded incredulous. "Like she had a type?"

Daniel frowned and put his hand on Ginger's. "Maybe. Or maybe something about her attracted the wrong kind of men." Daniel's voice was soft as he said those words and Sarah saw compassion in his eyes.

Sarah took a big gulp of wine, popped a piece of dark chocolate Santa boot into her mouth, and chewed. After she swallowed, she remarked to the room, "I wonder if Maurice is like the others." She tried to picture it, but all she could see was him sobbing on the swing set, seeming completely destroyed because Fiona was gone. Maybe Fiona had figured out a way to break the cycle. Sarah hoped that was the case.

Ginger asked, "Did you find anything else?"

Jared said, "Maurice's last name is Kingsley."

Sarah interrupted, "Oh, that's right I knew that. He said so the day I found Fiona."

"Well you didn't tell us." Jared laughed. "And he and Fiona have lived in Cedar Rapids, Lincoln, and Lubbock together. She has lived in a dozen other places besides those, and he's lived mostly in Texas until they cohabitated elsewhere."

Daniel added, "I wrote down all of the addresses we could find. There's also a website for the candy shop with information about her on it. She called herself a chocolatier."

"Interesting," Sarah said. "When I went past there the other morning, Maurice was putting packaged chocolates into the baskets. So I mentally questioned if they made them or bought them and resold them. I wonder where they made the products, since it didn't seem to be at the store."

"No idea,' Daniel said.

"I'm gonna go there tomorrow," Ginger said. "I'll offer to sell his line in the cafe in case he'd rather focus on his grooming business. What do you think? That will also give me an excuse to talk to him."

"It's a nice gesture," Sarah said. "But be careful. I mean, he seems all broken up and everything, but in my head I hear Chief James' voice reminding us we don't know if he's a killer—or not."

"Point taken. I'll be careful." Ginger finished the wine in her glass and then she stretched. "It's almost midnight and I have to be up in three and a half hours."

"You guys can crash here if you want. Jared can bunk with me," Sarah offered, noticing Jared's eyes sparkling at the suggestion.

Ginger shook her head no. "I love you both, but I need my own bed. Come on, Danny-boy, let's get going." She stood and reached for his hand to pull him up. He placed a soft kiss on her lips and then tugged her toward the door.

"Drive safely, and sleep well for as long as you can." Sarah locked the door behind them.

"I can still bunk with you," Jared suggested.

Sarah paused, thinking she liked the sound of that, but she was worried about his cuts, bruises, and broken leg. What if she thrashed in a bad dream and hit him? She'd feel horrible.

"I see your hesitation," Jared said, pressing his lips to hers in a sweet kiss. "Another time perhaps." He wished her goodnight and hobbled into his room.

"I don't want to hurt you in my sleep," she said to his retreating back.

He stopped in his doorway and turned to look at her. "I get it, Sarah. It's okay. There will be plenty of time for us."

"Thank you for understanding," she said, ushering Whiskey toward their bedroom. She was glad he didn't have to be at Java and Juice for six hours. She set her alarm for five-forty-five planning to not even exit her Jeep as she dropped him off.

At eight the next morning, after four cups of coffee, which was two more than she normally drank, Sarah told Emily about her night, feeling relief that she could finally fill Emily in on what really happened to Fiona.

"Holy crap, Sarah. You found the murder weapon?" Emily tied the denim dog print apron behind her. The extensions were gone and the spikes in her hair were a bit deflated today and her coloring was almost as pale at Taylor's.

Sarah wondered if Emily was coming down with the flu, but she didn't want to ask or point out how bad her assistant looked. "Maybe." Sarah took the brushes out of the cleaning solution, rinsed and dried them, and set them on the trays so they'd be ready to use. "They need to run some DNA tests to see if the blood and particles are a match."

Emily grimaced and said, "Yeah, but how many other people have been bludgeoned in the back of the head in this town in the past week? Was there hair in what you saw? What color was it?"

"Since when do you use words like bludgeoned?" Sarah joked. "Are you watching the True Crime Network?"

"No, a cold case podcast." Emily flipped the sign on the door to open. "And you didn't answer the question."

"The brief bits of what could have been hair were embedded in dark, dried blood so I couldn't really tell. Plus, it was dark outside, a bit overcast, and everything seemed to happen so fast. First, I almost fell flat on my face into the mess, then when I reached down to see what made me unstable and I realized what it was, it took some doing to get it free from its burial. John came almost as soon as we called."

"Did you look this morning to see if the Dumpster or area behind the pop-up shop is cordoned off? Any police tape? It's garbage day. I would think the police wouldn't let the city empty that one."

"I didn't drive or walk past there this morning. It was all I could handle, taking Jared to work, walking and feeding Whiskey, mainlining caffeine, and getting myself here on time. I'm not a person who can function on five hours of sleep."

"I hear you." Emily giggled like an elementary schooler with a crush.

Sarah raised her eyebrows in question.

"I may not have gotten much sleep myself," Emily admitted. "After dinner we caught a late movie and then we played video games almost until the sun came up. We had so much fun and were online with players all over the world. But now I'm paying the price. I'll need to run to Java and Juice for more coffee." She took a sip from her black to-go cup and then frowned. "It's empty."

"Go. Go now before our first two clients get here." Just as Sarah said that, the Coiffure's green front door opened and in walked Sascha with her head held high, followed by Barbara Order, wearing a puffy white parka over purple yoga tights.

Whiskey let loose a friendly "woof" and trotted over to nip at his friend's neck, his way of saying, "Come on, let's play."

Barbara let go of Sascha's leash and it trailed behind the dog as she romped with Whiskey.

"Good morning, Mrs. Order," Emily said, easing past her and out the door.

"Coffee run," Sarah explained.

"James got back to the house two hours ago, thanks to your discovery," Barbara said. "I left him snoring and took over the errands he was planning to run. Any chance you can keep Sascha here until noon when you close?"

"Absolutely. Whiskey would love that. We could even drop him off on our way home if it is easier for you and the chief today."

"That's so sweet of you. Here, let me pay you in advance for his grooming and we'll see you this afternoon. I appreciate your offer, Sarah." Barbara handed Sarah a credit card and signed the receipt and then left after hugging Sascha around the neck and telling her to be a good girl.

"Come on, beautiful, let's get you in the tub." Sarah opened the door on one of the walk-in stainless steel tubs, and Sascha stepped right in. Whiskey leaned against the side of the tub to provide emotional support. They were mid-shampoo when the door opened again and Emily returned with a full to-go cup, plus two espresso-, chocolate-, and raspberry-filled croissants and two bear claws the size of grizzlies' paws.

"Fat, caffeine, and sugar, just what the doctor ordered," Emily joked, setting everything on the table in the back. "Officer Grimes was at the cafe. She said to give you the message that she'll be by in a professional capacity in about an hour." Emily sunk her teeth into the bear claw and purred. She closed her eyes as she chewed, clearly enjoying the yeasty dough, the cinnamon, almond paste, and raisins.

Sarah rinsed the suds from both layers of Sascha's fur until the water ran clear, and then she led the German shepherd to a grooming table that stood two feet from the ground and asked her to jump up. Sascha landed with the grace of a ballerina.

By the time Emily finished her pastries, a five-pound chihuahua named Peanut had been dropped off for a bath and nail trim. She gently tended to the tiny dog in the tub, keeping the water pressure at a soft trickle. Peanut shivered and shook, his large eyes wide with mistrust as he tried to balance on his tiny paws, looking up at Emily with a mix of nervousness and hope for rescue.

Emily cooed at him and whispered, "It's okay, it's okay," on repeat before stating, "There. We are almost done." She turned off the water and wrapped the timid beast in a fluffy bath towel with only his small head peeking out from the folds. She gathered him against her chest and rubbed him through the towel until he stopped shivering. Then she set him on the table, still in the towel, but pulled out one of his feet to trim the tips of his nails.

"Remind me to recommend to his human that she buy him a sweater or two. He really shouldn't be outside without one. He has little body fat and his fur is much too thin for our weather."

"Sure, Sarah. And when I'm done here, I'll pick out a few for her to choose from. I love the red and white snowflake sweater and I think there's still one in Peanut's size left from the Winter Wonderland stock."

"Sounds good," Sarah said, brushing Sascha's long tail.

The bell on the green door jingled and Whiskey raced to greet the newcomer, who turned out to be Officer Candace Grimes decked out in her Class B wool uniform with tactical black boots. "Hello, Whiskey," she greeted. "Sarah, Emily." She tipped her hat to them.

Sarah tied a hunter green with clumps of tiny red holly berries bandana around Sascha's neck and then allowed her to jump to the floor. She, too, ran to greet Officer Grimes before putting her open mouth on Whiskey's neck to get him to chase her.

Sarah opened the counter and walked through, meeting Candace in the waiting area. "Beams wrote this up last night, err, early this morning. I need you to read it, let me know if anything is missing or incorrect, and if it all looks good to sign it."

Sarah read through John's report and her statement. It was all accurate, but she was surprised to see a note saying she and Ginger would not be charged with trespassing. "Um, it looks fine," Sarah mumbled. "Give me the pen and I'll sign."

Candace had known Sarah for almost six years and they were friends so Sarah's deflation of energy was transparent. "That trespassing comment hurt your feelings?"

"I mean, why would they even consider that, considering what I found?"

"They didn't. It was a CYA in case the property owner wants to press charges or turns out to be the suspect and wants to get revenge on you that way, by suing you for trespassing."

"Oh. Then tell John thanks, I guess."

"Just doing our jobs. By the way, the driver of the truck that hit Jared, he had a fatal heart attack, which is why he could no longer control the rig. I thought you'd want to know."

"Oh my gosh. His poor family," Sarah said. "And so close to Christmas."

Officer Grimes nodded. "I let Jared know this morning. He looks like he's doing well."

"He is. He's still staying with me so he has a ride to work and back. At least I think that's why." Sarah smirked.

"Yeah, I'm sure that's it." Sarcasm dripped from her words as Grimes gave Sarah a knowing look.

"Oh stop." Sarah swatted at Candace.

"Are you trying to assault an officer of the law? I'll have you arrested, girl." Grimes teased, her guffaw filling the room.

"Hey." Sarah changed the subject. "If we get through these next couple of weeks, I'm hosting an informal party on December 23. If you're off, come and celebrate with us, any time after six. Bring whomever you want. And that includes Maple."

"Sounds good. Well, I've gotta go. Duty calls. Bye, Emily." And with that Grimes was out the door.

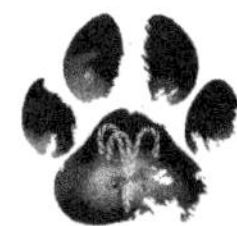

CHAPTER EIGHTEEN

It was twelve-thirty by the time Sarah made it to Java and Juice to pick up Jared. Whiskey welcomed him with a slurp to the cheek as Jared slid on the passenger seat of the Jeep "Hey, Sarah, can we go to that chocolate pop-up before we go home?"

"You didn't get enough chocolate last night?"

"Actually, I wanted to get a bunch of naughty elves to send to my brother. He'll find those hilarious."

"Oh. Do you have any other shopping you need help with? I mean, I have the afternoon free. We can go get the wheelchair or I can drive us to the mall." The closest mall was thirty minutes away.

Jared shook his head. His green eyes looked more sunken than usual, like the lack of sleep had caught up with him. "I do have gifts to buy, but I'll do it later. I just figured since we were out and the shop is only a few blocks away and I have never been..." His voice trailed off.

"And you'd like to see the scene of the crime?" Sarah filled in.

"Um, kind of. Though you said that was the backroom and I'd have no reason to go back there."

"Not unless you faked a bathroom emergency." Sarah drove around the block to get to the candy store since she had been traveling northbound on Main instead of southbound. A car pulled out just as she approached and Sarah easily slid the CJ into the space right in front.

Jared had the passenger door open before Sarah turned off the engine. "Stay here, Whiskey," he said before shutting his door.

Sarah repeated Jared's instructions to her dog and went to open the front door of the store so Jared could enter. No one was manning the register, which surprised Sarah. She wondered if Maurice ran to the back for more candy as the place seemed to be busy. At least a dozen customers were in the small space, including Hannah Beau and her two adopted Chinese daughters, Bao and Ai. The five-year-old girls greeted Sarah as soon as they saw her.

"Sarah," they squealed. "Where's Whiskey?" they asked in stereo.

She bent and hugged them one by one. "He's in the car outside. Chocolate is dangerous to dogs."

"Like Brussel sprouts are to me," Bao insisted.

"Um, not quite like that. While you may not like Brussel sprouts, eating them won't actually kill you," Sarah said, still squatting at child level.

"That's what you think," Bao giggled.

"Stop being silly," Ai said. "We need to pick out some chocolate for Daddy's stocking. But shhhh, Sarah, it's a secret." Ai put her finger to her lips in a gesture Sarah realized she must be mimicking from Hannah.

"Your secret is safe with me," Sarah promised. "It's good to see you both." She looked up to see Jared trying to balance standing, holding his crutches, holding and opening the mesh bag, and putting chocolate choices inside. He didn't look too stable so she rushed to his side to take over the holding and opening of the bag.

"Thanks," he said, being selective in the elves he chose for his brother. "These are so funny." He showed Sarah a female elf in stilettos dancing on a pole.

Sarah glanced up as Maurice emerged from the backroom, his index finger wiping under his nose. She watched Hannah approach the register with her girls, and Maurice offered them sample pieces of milk chocolate. Bao and Ai grinned and bounced on the balls of their feet, clearly excited, but Sarah noticed Hannah's smile was tight, like she didn't approve of something about Maurice. Sarah said goodbye to them as they exited the store.

"I'm ready now," Jared said, indicating that Sarah should take his bag to the register as he maneuvered around the tables and displays, some of which were tight for someone on crutches.

When they got to the front table, Maurice greeted Sarah with a hello. Recognition shown in his red eyes. "How are you?" Sarah asked, keeping her voice low. His eyes looked odd to her, but she didn't immediately understand why. It was not because of the bloodshot whites.

"Been better," Maurice said. "Thank you for your kindness the other morning." He told Jared the total and ran Jared's credit card.

"I'm sorry for your loss," Sarah said.

As they turned and walked to the door, which Sarah held open for Jared, she realized what was gnawing at her. She glanced back at Maurice who was helping another customer, but he made eye contact with her as he said, "Thank you for your business." The pupils of his eyes were constricted so much they almost disappeared into pinpricks, barely visible against the dark irises. Sarah's stomach flipped as the realization settled in—something wasn't right. His voice had been calm, almost too calm, but those eyes... they looked wrong, unnatural, like he was suppressing something deep within.

As she stepped outside with Jared, the cold air hit her face, but her mind was still back in the store. She had seen eyes like that before—when a childhood friend had a traumatic brain injury after a metal rack at a department store collapsed and one of the hooks embedded in her skull, changing her for life. Unease gripped her. Even though she didn't really know him, she hoped Maurice would be okay. Losing someone you loved was always difficult, but losing someone you loved so close to the holidays took the loss to a whole different level.

When they got to Sarah's house, she suggested they eat some leftover lasagna for lunch and then if Jared wasn't too tired, she would love his help decorating her house and tree. In all of the busyness since Jared's accident, the preparation for Winter Wonderland, and the extended hours of the Coiffure for the holidays, Sarah hadn't had any bandwidth or time to drag her artificial tree or boxes of trimming down from the attic. Nor had she baked any holiday treats, including the Scottish shortbread cookies or thumbprint cookies Gigi had taught her to make.

"I'd love to help you decorate," Jared said. "But what I'd love even more is if we could eat and then take a nap first. I'm not even sure how I made it through the day. The lack of sleep is slamming into me right now. And I've done too much. I need to put my leg up and rest." He collapsed into the first chair he came to in the living room.

Sarah kissed the top of his head. "Of course. You've been through so much. I'll reheat the food and bring it to you. We can eat in here."

Whiskey followed Sarah into the kitchen to see if she planned to feed him. She handed him a dehydrated chicken breast chew. He chomped it and ran into the living room to lay on the rug and eat it. Sarah put two helpings of lasagna on a plate and a no-splatter lid on top of it and placed it in the microwave. She pulled two plates from the cupboard and plopped salad onto half of each plate and sprinkled some olive oil and balsamic over it, and then when the microwave finished doing its thing, placed a serving of the lasagna next to the salad.

By the time she brought the food into the living room, she found Jared fast asleep with his neck craned backwards resting against the top of the chair. His mouth was open, which she found comical. She was tempted to run her finger over his bottom lip.

She controlled her impulse and instead said softly, "Jared, lunch is ready."

He didn't respond.

Louder, she said the words again and touched his arm. He jerked and his eyes popped open and his mouth shut.

"Eat and then we'll nap on the bed together. It will be way more comfortable than that chair." She sat at the end of the love seat near him and handed him his plate.

After a few bites of food she said, "Did Maurice look okay to you?"

"I don't know," Jared said. "I've never seen him before, so I don't know what he usually looks like. His eyes were red like he had been crying. But that's understandable. I'd cry an ocean if something happened to you."

"Good to know," Sarah said. She gave him a small smile, appreciating the sentiment, but she still felt unsettled. She pushed her food around on her plate, her appetite fading. "Yeah, but it wasn't just that," she murmured, more to herself than to Jared. "His pupils...they were tiny. I don't know why, but it really bugs me."

Jared glanced up from his plate. "Tiny pupils? Maybe he's on some kind of medication. Or it could just be stress, Sarah. He did just lose someone."

"Maybe..." Sarah's voice trailed off, but something deep inside told her there was more to it than just grief.

Two hours later after a dreamless nap with the three of them on the bed together, one of Gigi's crocheted afghans over Sarah and Jared, and with Whiskey curled at their feet, they awoke to the shrill of the doorbell. Whiskey launched himself from the room, barking like intruders were trying to enter.

Sarah stretched before planting her feet on the floor and yelled, "I'm coming."

She looked out the peephole and spied Helen Goode in her postal uniform holding a brown wrapped package the size of a shoe box.

"Hi, Helen. Happy holidays." Sarah had opened the door wide and Whiskey sniffed Helen's shoe.

"Hello, Whiskey." She pulled a Milk Bone from her uniform pocket and held it in front of his snout. "Merry Christmas to you, Sarah. Looks like someone sent you good cheer." Helen's brown eyes radiated warmth and kindness.

"My goodness. Thank you very much." Sarah took the box and the mail that was piled on top of it. "Do you have time for a cup of tea?"

"Not today. I'm covering part of my colleague's territory as he took the day off. So I'm running behind. Have a great evening."

"Thank you. You too." Sarah shut the door and walked into the kitchen and placed the stack of mail on the counter. She grabbed a box cutter from a drawer, set the cards and bills aside, and froze when she saw the precise all capital letter address in black Sharpie on the outside of the box. The word FRAGILE had been written in red ink.

"Jared," she screamed. "Get in here." Her whole body was vibrating in fear. Unlike the letters, this package was delivered to her home. The sender knew where she lived. Her chest tightened and she couldn't breathe.

The ka-klunk ka-klunk of Jared's crutches could be heard coming from the bedroom. "What? What is it? What's going on?" he asked, moving toward her as fast as he could.

Sarah had her phone pressed to her ear. "Come on, come on, come on. Answer." She mumbled into the phone. Anxiety tightened around her like a vise. Her hands shook as she gripped the phone, waiting for the call to connect. "Please, pick up," she whispered, her voice barely audible.

Jared, still a few feet away, saw the box on the counter and his expression darkened. "Is it another one?" he asked, his voice low and laced with concern.

Sarah nodded, her breath coming in shallow gasps. "But this time...it's here. At my home," she managed to say, the panic in her voice unmistakable.

Jared reached her side, placing a hand on her trembling shoulder. "Are you calling the police?"

"The chief," Sarah answered, her eyes never leaving the box. "This is different, Jared. It's not like the letters at work. They know where I live. They are making that clear."

Jared's grip tightened on his crutch. "We'll figure this out, okay? You're not alone in this."

"I feel so violated." The chief's phone went to voicemail so Sarah ended the call. She found Officer Beams in her contacts and called him.

He answered on the second ring. "Hi, Sarah."

"I need you...at my house...now. I tried the chief. He didn't answer—"

He cut her off. "Yeah, he and Barbara went away for the night. It's their anniversary. I've got Sascha with me."

"Both of you need to come here. Helen just brought the mail and in it was a package...from the letter sender."

"What's in it?"

"No idea. I don't want to open it. What if it's a bomb or contains anthrax or something? He said he was coming for me."

"Don't touch or move anything. I'll be right there. Hang tight. On second thought, grab your coats and Whiskey and get the hell out of your house. Stay out and stand at least across the street and wait for me."

"Uh, okay." Beams' instructions reinforced how real the situation was.

Sarah raced around grabbing her boots, coat, gloves, and hat, Whiskey's leash, and the keys to her Jeep—which she then moved and parked up the street—and a bag with her computer and Jared's in it.

As they stood across the street awaiting the arrival of John Beams, the fire department, and whomever else was acting as the calvary, Mrs. Jenkins popped out of her front door. "Sarah, is everything all right?"

"Ummm, maybe you should go to Gladys'. I got a suspicious package and have been receiving threats so the police are on their way. Officer Beams asked us to evacuate the house."

"That sounds serious," Mrs. Jenkins said. She was in her usual pastel tweed suit, cream colored shell, with pearls around her neck, looking like she was headed to tea with the Queen. "Did you hear any ticking?"

Sarah paused and thought about the answer to the question. "No. I believe the box was silent."

"Anything like grease or powder on the box?"

Sarah pursed her lips. She hadn't inspected the package. As soon as she saw the recognizable writing, she went into action. "I didn't see any."

Mrs. Jenkins nodded her head. "I'm glad you didn't try to open it. Best to leave those things to the professionals." She gave Sarah a knowing smile. "Would you and your gentlemen like to come in?"

"No, thank you. We'll wait out here."

CHAPTER NINETEEN

Officer Beams' tires screeched as he took the turn onto Sarah's street a little too fast. Sirens wailed and were coming closer. John slammed his car to a stop in front of Robert Wise's house and hoofed it down the hill toward Sarah. "Your house is empty, right? Hello, Janice."

"Yes." Sarah said. Whiskey thumped his tail on the sidewalk next to her in response to seeing John, whom he considered a friend.

"Hi, John," Mrs. Jenkins said.

"Is the door unlocked?"

"Yes."

The red fire truck pulled to the curb behind John's car. Two firefighters wearing hazmat suits stepped out of the cab. "Did you call the county bomb squad?"

"They said they were at another call and would be a while, maybe an hour. I called a friend, a detonation specialist, instead." John pointed at an older sedan pulling to the curb behind the fire truck.

Sarah was surprised to see Bill getting out of the car.

"Bill. Thank you for being available," Beams said.

"Sure. Sure. Glad I can use my expertise after all of this time. Where's the package?"

The firefighters, Officer Beams, and Bill were all looking at Sarah, but she didn't notice since she was still in shock over seeing Bill. Jared answered, "On her kitchen counter. Hey, thanks for saving me." He acknowledged one of the firefighters who had held the bookcase while the Parks pulled him out. The male firefighter smiled but remained silent.

"Huh? Oh yeah, right. On my kitchen counter," Sarah said.

"Then let's go," Bill said, crossing the street carrying what looked like a toolbox.

One of the two firefighters carried a black backpack while the other carried something with a canister, but its shape reminded Sarah of a movie camera. Officer Beams told Sarah, Jared, and Whiskey to stay right where they were.

Mrs. Jenkins explained, "Bill was a demolition expert in the military. If that package has an explosive, he'll figure it out and deal with it. But that thing the firefighter was carrying, that was a portable x-ray machine. I'm guessing a laptop, cables, and a shield were in the backpack."

"So, Cottageville doesn't have a bomb team?" Jared asked.

"Too small," Mrs. Jenkins said. "That's why they rely on the county, just like for the crime lab."

"Makes sense," Jared said, moving to sit on the front steps of Mrs. Jenkins' house.

"Is your leg hurting?" Sarah asked.

"Too much standing."

Sarah looked longingly at her home, her inheritance from Gigi. Tears filled her eyes when she registered how easily it could all disappear—with a bomb, a natural gas explosion, arson. She told herself that people not things mattered, but she loved her home and things that were passed down and the traditions she had been able to carry on in her grandmother's memory. And she'd be damned if she'd let some invisible person who was determined to make her fearful screw that up. She balled her hands into fists like she was ready for a fight and set her jaw, her heart pounding with a mixture of terror and defiance. Sarah wiped away the tears before they could fall, forcing herself to take a deep breath. "No one's taking this from me," she whispered under her breath, her voice steely with determination.

The house wasn't just walls and a roof; it was her connection to Gigi, the memories, the warmth of family traditions, the safety of belonging somewhere that was truly hers. She had fought too hard to keep that connection alive, and she wasn't about to let it slip away because of fear—because of *them*.

Jared watched her quietly, sensing the shift in her energy. "We'll handle this, Sarah. We'll figure out who's behind it."

She nodded, more to herself than to him. "We have to. I won't let them win."

With renewed resolve, she was ready—ready to face whatever, or whoever, was trying to push her into a corner.

The front door of her house opened inward and out came the firefighter with the backpack carrying the box, which was still unopened. He was followed by Bill, Officer Beams, and the firefighter with the x-ray machine. They stopped in front of Mrs. Jenkins' house and addressed Sarah and her friends.

John Beams said, "We have good news and bad news. The box contains not a bomb nor any type of explosive device. It also doesn't seem to contain any powder."

Sarah let out a breath she didn't realize she was holding, and Jared reached up and squeezed her hand.

"But," Beams continued, "the x-ray showed...um...organic matter...." His voice trailed off.

"Recognizable organic matter, John?" Mrs. Jenkins asked.

"Indeed. It seems you've been sent a box of turds, Sarah."

"Holy—" Jared started to say before John interrupted with "Exactly."

"We're going to send the whole thing to the county and let them dismantle it and process it. I'll let you know if they find a note and what it says. In the meantime, please talk to your neighbors and let them know what's been going on and to keep their eyes open for anything or anyone suspicious. And do not go anywhere by yourself until we make an arrest. Things are clearly escalating, so take precautions."

"I will," Sarah promised. "Thank you. I'm so grateful this has turned out the way it did." A tear trickled down her cheek. She knew part of this was the after-adrenaline effects, but the other part was feeling cared for by Bill, John, Mrs. Jenkins, and Jared, and even the two firefighters Sarah had never met.

After the police car and fire trucks pulled away from the curb, Mrs. Jenkins invited everyone inside her house as the temperature was near freezing. Bill, Whiskey, Jared, Sarah filed one by one on the way in as Robert Wise took that moment to shuffle down the sidewalk in his black turtleneck, red cardigan, black wool pants, and his black leather moccasin style slippers to his next door neighbor's. "What happened? What'd I miss?"

Mrs. Jenkins invited him inside too, and they all sat on sofas and chairs in her living room, and Whiskey curled on the floor next to Sarah's foot. Sarah figured now was as good a time as any to take Officer Beams' advice. She told those gathered the story of the threats received at the Coiffure, showed them pictures of the second letter and envelope, and ended with the arrival of this afternoon's package of poop.

Robert wrinkled his nose and said, "Eww, gross."

"Agreed," Sarah said, "But it could have been so much worse. Bill, I had no idea you are an explosives expert. I'm sure you've got some incredible stories."

His blue-gray eyes sparkled in the porch lights. "The army trained me, and when I got out, mining companies and the Department of Transportation needed my skills. But somewhere along the way I grew into a person who couldn't stand the destruction of the landscape, the way beautiful mountains were decimated all in the name of progress." He grimaced. "It's why I went back to school to study earth sciences and became a teacher. I wanted to instill awe and wonder for our natural world."

"That's amazing," Sarah said. "You're a good soul."

"Yes, he is," Janice Jenkins agreed, beaming at him in a way that squished the laugh lines around her eyes. "Sarah, do you have any thoughts as to who is targeting you and why?"

"Well, at first, I thought when the person said they were coming for me, they meant they were coming for my business. I wondered if it was that new mobile grooming business, that white van that's been parked all over the place. The guy's name is Maurice. But then..." She stopped because she wasn't sure if she should get into the candy pop-up drama. "Something happened to the health of his partner who ran that new chocolate shop on Main, and he's now taken over the running of that, so I don't think he's doing much dog grooming or that my business is much of a threat to him. So now I don't really know what to think."

"Is there any indication the person knows much about you?" Mrs. Jenkins asked.

Sarah could see her professional demeanor kicking in. Janice Jenkins must have been a very good federal agent back in the day. "The first note used the acronym COY, which I assumed meant Citizen of the Year, since the note arrived in a Christmas card just after I was given the key to the city by the mayor."

"And everything has had a Cottageville postmark?"

"Yes."

"So, it is clearly someone local. Have you made anyone angry recently?"

"I don't think so. Other than maybe George's chihuahua

Chutney, who loathes us with the fire of a thousand suns, to misquote Shakespeare and *Taming of the Shrew.*"

"That's not a dog's handwriting," Jared was quick to quip. "Plus I can't see him cutting out all of those letters without opposable thumbs."

"Definitely not," Sarah agreed.

Robert and Bill had remained silent through Janice's questions. But Bill spoke up, "Sarah, on Monday, you should go see Luella at the post office. I know the police will probably talk with her, but maybe show her the photo or share it with her and she can alert her staff so they can keep a lookout for anything addressed to you with no return address and that black all capital letter handwriting."

"That's a great idea, Bill," Janice said.

"I'll do that," Sarah said. "And I appreciate all of you keeping watch for me. We should probably get going, as I know Whiskey would like some dinner, and before all of this happened, I had planned to put up my Christmas tree tonight." Sarah stood so Whiskey stood, too. Jared pushed himself upright using his crutches.

"I'm here for you any time, Sarah. Please know that. And not just because you saved me." Mrs. Jenkins walked with them to her front door.

"I'll go now, too," Robert said, kissing Mrs. Jenkins' cheek. "Sarah, Mozart and I will keep an eye out, too. Take care of yourself and stay safe."

"That's the plan." Sarah hugged him goodbye, and she hugged Bill and Mrs. Jenkins, too. Then she, Jared, and Whiskey locked themselves inside her house.

Jared said, "You okay with grilled cheese and salad? I'll make us supper and feed Whiskey, if you want to start getting the boxes down."

Sarah stood on her tiptoes and kissed his cheek. "I would love that. Thank you." She grabbed the step ladder from the closet and opened it in the hallway right before her bedroom door. Then Sarah climbed the ladder and pushed the white painted piece of wood that served as the attic door. She angled it into the attic and then climbed into the space and hit the light switch. The boxes were a bit dusty and a few mouse droppings dotted the plywood flooring, but Sarah kept the attic well organized and relatively clean. She picked up three boxes, one at a time, of ornaments and decorations and carried them down the ladder and into the living room. And then she lugged a plastic tub of lights, and Whiskey, who must have finished his food, trotted alongside her from the ladder to the living room and back again. He kept watch with his front feet on the first step as she crawled back through the hole in the hallway ceiling. On the last trip down, she had the tree in its big, zippered dark green bag. She hit the switch with her elbow to turn off the light and then set the bag on the top of the ladder, while she stood a few steps down, securing the wooden door, just in case the mice were still up there.

Before she dug into the boxes or assembled the tree, Jared announced it was time to eat. Sarah met him in the kitchen to carry their plates to the table. "Thank you so much for this," Sarah said, when they were seated.

"My pleasure." Jared patted her hand. "I didn't want to get all emo in front of the police and the others, but I'm so happy you're okay, Sarah. And that your house is fine and that that wasn't a bomb. I can't wait until I get this cast off and can be better support for you." His moss green eyes bore into hers as he squeezed her hand gently, his expression a mix of relief and affection. "You've been through so much already," he continued, his voice soft but full of emotion. "I just want to be there for you the way you've been there for me."

Sarah's heart warmed at his words, but she could still feel the lingering tension in her chest. She met his gaze, his eyes searching hers for reassurance. "You are supporting me, Jared," she said, her voice steady. "I don't need you to be able to run or fight for me. Just being here—knowing you're by my side—is more than enough."

Jared smiled, though the worry still lingered behind his eyes. "I mean it, though. Once I'm back on my feet, I'm going to make sure we get through this together. No more fear."

Sarah nodded, her hand still in his, feeling the weight of his promise. "Together," she whispered, feeling just a little bit lighter in that moment.

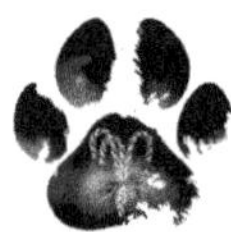

CHAPTER TWENTY

Saturday night after they ate, Sarah had pieced together her realistic looking but artificial Fraser fir and its tiny white lights that made it sparkle like stars in the night sky. The glow from the tree filled the room with a warm, comforting ambiance, softening the edges of her worries, if only for a moment. Each ornament she hung felt like a small act of defiance against the chaos that had recently invaded her life. The tree, with its twinkling lights and cherished decorations, was a reminder of tradition, of normalcy, of the life she had fought so hard to maintain.

Christmas music from a streaming service played through a portable speaker as she occasionally sang along and as Jared watched her from the couch, his leg propped up, with Whiskey stretched out with his spine against Jared's cast. "It looks beautiful," he said.

Sarah stepped back, taking in the full view of the tree. It was perfect, even if it wasn't real. "Thanks." She smiled. "I guess I needed this, something to hold onto."

Jared nodded. "We both do." The twinkle of the lights danced in his eyes, and for a moment, it felt like the world outside didn't matter—like they were safe, together with Whiskey in their little bubble of light and warmth. She walked to him and gave him a kiss that turned slightly steamy before she broke away, grinning and flushed, and went back to decorating the tree.

When she had most of the ornaments on the fir and was taking out Whiskey's giant red felt paw shaped stocking from a box along with the red, kelly green, and white one Gigi had knit her during her childhood, Jared asked, "Would you like some hot chocolate? We still have those fancy marshmallows from the pop-up shop."

"Yum. I'd love some."

Jared heaved himself off the sofa as Whiskey opened his eyes to see where his friend was going. When Jared's back was to her, Sarah opened an app on her phone and searched for a stocking for him. She figured he might still be at her house through Christmas so she wanted to be prepared. She found an artist who made personalized ones to order and promised it would arrive before the holiday so Sarah ordered it before Jared returned with their drinks, and a chicken chew for his favorite red heeler.

Sarah sat on the sofa with her guys, taking a break, and sipping on the rich, dark, and marshmallowy drink. "This is so good."

"It is. Can you get more of these marshmallows tomorrow?"

"Sure thing. If he's open. Do you want any chocolates or fireballs or any candy?" Sarah planned to get some candy and naughty elves to put in his stocking.

"I'd never say no to chocolate." He grinned at her.

The next morning while drinking a cup of black coffee and while Jared was in the bath, Sarah called Ginger and told her about the package and the new knowledge she had about Bill. Her bestie's fury at the sender was immediate and palpable. "What the hell, Sarah?" Ginger nearly shouted over the phone. "Who does this jerk think they are? Sending that package to your home—that's crossing the line."

Sarah could almost see Ginger pacing back and forth, her fiery temper bubbling over. "I know, it's terrifying," Sarah said, her voice low as she cradled the mug in her hands. "But I think the line was crossed by sending the first note. This was a form of escalation."

"Yeah, escalation of my rage. Are you okay? How can you be calm about this?"

Sarah heard water running like Ginger was filling a water glass. "I'm calm because it wasn't an explosive and I've had a night to recover. Christmas music and decorating and being grateful for all of my memories as I unwrapped each ornament has a way of bringing tempers and fear down a few notches. And then Jared made the best hot chocolate using homemade marshmallows from the pop-up shop. That reminds me, I told him I'd pick up more of those today. Have you been yet? Do you want to come?"

"I haven't been, even though I've thought about asking the dude if he wanted Java to carry his products. I just got so busy. I'd love to go with you. Daniel's working today. Actually, if I can get us appointments, can we go get our brows done before or after getting marshmallows? I've got a forest over my eyes that needs to be thinned."

"Aww. I didn't notice that when you were here Friday night."

"It's true."

"Okay. I'll go with you to that if you come to the store with me. Wait, let me check online if they are even open." Sarah used the browser on her tablet to pull up the store's website. "Says they open at noon. Text me when you find out if we can get wax appointments."

"Will do." They disconnected, and Sarah poked around the pop-up shop's website, learning all she could about Fiona and her training. Sarah noticed a calendar of where the pop-up had been and noted that it would be moving on to Kansas City the first week of January. Maurice Kingsley was mentioned nowhere on the site.

Sarah did a Google search on "Fiona Fiore" and besides the court documents Daniel and Jared mentioned, she saw social media pages that had photos of Fiona and her Stetson-wearing cowboy. In all of the photos Fiona's face glowed with joy and love. *Maybe she had met her Prince Charming,* Sarah thought.

Her phone pinged with a message from Ginger. "I could only get one waxing appointment for today and I need it more than you. Still want to join me?"

Sarah responded, "Do they still serve complimentary mimosas with every service?"

"Yes."

"I'm in. What time?"

"I'll swing by at 11:30."

"K."

Sarah heard the water start draining from the tub. She poured coffee into a mug with Whiskey's picture on the front—the mug Jared had used every morning since he had moved in—and added a splash of extra creamy oat milk, just how he liked it. She set it on the counter and pulled eggs, feta, spinach, and cherry tomatoes from the fridge. She had a skillet heating and a pat of butter melting before Jared made it into the kitchen. "My turn to make breakfast," she said. "Take a seat at the counter and keep me company."

"My pleasure." Jared took his first mouthful of coffee.

"I'm going out for an hour with Ginger to do girl things and we'll pick up those marshmallows. Need anything else while I'm out?"

"No. I'm going to do online Christmas shopping and I have some cards I want to write and send. Plus, Whiskey and I will watch some football." At his name, Whiskey picked up his head from where he had been lying on the kitchen floor. He looked at Jared and smiled like the idea of watching a pigskin get thrown around appealed to him.

Sarah cut the big omelet she made onto two plates that were already embellished with buttered sourdough toast triangles. She passed a plate and a fork to Jared and she stood across the counter from him and they ate.

Afterward, Sarah strung colored holiday lights around the porch railing of her craftsman bungalow and placed an evergreen and holly berry wreath on a hanger on her front door. In the backyard, she and Whiskey clipped some skinny branches from a Serbian spruce tree and used those to decorate her fireplace mantel before placing cylindrical red pillar candles amongst the greenery.

"Wow. That smells amazing," Jared said, resting again on the sofa with his leg up. "Just like a Christmas forest." His eyes sparkled as he grinned.

"Hey, since you might be here through the holidays, are there any decorations you want to get from your place and add to the mix?"

"That's so sweet," Jared said. "Let me think about it."

At that moment Ginger's SUV pulled into Sarah's driveway and Whiskey alerted with a single bark. Sarah kissed Jared on his lips and said she'd be back soon. "Stick with G," he reminded "and lock the front door behind you please so I don't have to get up."

"I will." Sarah, clad in black yoga pants and a "just a girl who loves dogs" sweatshirt, pushed her arms into her navy puffy jacket, pushed her feet into Uggs, and grabbed her hat and scarf and then went out the door.

As soon as she got into the SUV, Ginger said, "I can't believe someone sent you poop. So gross." Ginger's blonde hair was in two braids again, which was almost her signature look, and she wore a thermal shirt under overalls and a dark green puffy jacket, open down the front.

"That's better than anthrax?" Sarah raised her eyebrows.

"I'm not sure it is," Ginger countered.

"It's less deadly."

"Well, there is that. Thanks for spending time with me today and watching me torture myself with hot wax."

"I'm in it for the champagne. Oh, and moral support, of course."

"Of course." Ginger chuckled. "So, is everything going well with Mr. Crutchalong?"

"He's very easy to get along with," Sarah said as they drove north of town to a small strip mall that housed a donut shop, a wireless phone company, and Siren's Salon that specialized in facials, mani-pedis, and brows. Sergio's salon also did brows but they charged twice as much as Siren's. A space was available right in front of the salon so Ginger pulled in and parked and as soon as they entered, they were whisked to the back and offered flutes of champagne splashed with their choice of orange juice, grapefruit juice, or festive cranberry juice.

They toasted their friendship before Ginger was head back in a reclining chair, with a cloth strap holding her blonde bangs from her face while the esthetician inspected her eyebrows. The short dark haired woman wearing a white medical looking smock tsked, "So many stragglers." She applied a coat of wax under Ginger's brow line and then checked its stickiness with her finger before ripping it off. And then she repeated on the other side, on the tops of both brows, and then above Ginger's nose and between her brows, before pulling the last few stubborn hairs out with tweezers.

Sarah mentally questioned the things women did in the name of beauty. She wondered how waxing even started in the first place. *Why did someone decide this was a good idea?*

They finished the rest of their drinks, paid, and were on their way, with the skin around Ginger's eyes slightly pink from the procedure.

"I feel so much better now." She started the car and they headed back toward downtown. The sky was blue with white puffy clouds and the sun was shining, trying to raise the temperature above thirty-six degrees. A small herd of deer grazed in a field to Sarah's right and she pointed them out to Ginger.

"They look so serene," Sarah said, "just munching away."

"Don't kid yourself. With those big ears, they are always on high alert for any sounds of danger. Haven't you seen them run away like the devil is after them at the sound of a dog bark or footsteps crunching leaves? They are fast."

"Yes, but they seem so gentle."

"They are, but farmers also think they are a destructive nuisance. Not unlike the raccoon we saw the other night."

Sarah sighed, "I guess anything could be a nuisance if it eats your livelihood or destroys something you care about."

"Yep."

"We have the best luck with parking today," Sarah remarked as a space was open directly next to the Moe's Mobile Grooming van in front of the pop-up shop. Maurice exited the driver's side door of the van as Ginger pulled in. He moved to the front door with keys in his hand and unlocked it. Sarah glanced at her phone to see the time. Ten minutes after twelve. She guessed he was running late today.

They exited the SUV and walked to the store where he was inside turning on the lights. Sarah opened the door and asked before they entered, "Are you open or do you need a few minutes?"

Maurice's dark eyes showed little life and registered no recognition when he looked at Sarah, which Sarah thought was very strange. "I need to restock, but feel free to look around." He walked through the door that led to the backroom.

Sarah grabbed a mesh bag and added half a dozen elves in all varieties of naughtiness and then threw in a couple of bags of reindeer poop before pulling them back out of her bag and putting them back into the bushel. *Too close to home,* she decided, thinking about yesterday's package.

She eyed some white chocolate Santas and a dark chocolate and white chocolate painted snowman, and then inspected a commercially packaged box of truffles. Maurice came from the back with a tower of boxes and started filling in bushels, literally tossing candy into the baskets.

"Do you have any marshmallows in those boxes?" Sarah asked. "They are the best I've ever eaten, but the bin here is almost empty." Sarah held up the bushel in front of her so he could see.

"Uh, yeah, hang on." Maurice speedwalked behind the door again and not even a minute had gone by when he returned with a handful of packaged marshmallows. "This enough?"

Ginger eyed him. "I'd like some too, please."

He thrusted the ones in his hand into Sarah's bag and left the room to fill Ginger's order. "Mr. Personality," Ginger mumbled near Sarah's ear.

"He's suffered a loss," Sarah stuck up for him.

"I don't think it's that," Ginger whispered before turning a smile toward Maurice as he came out with two handfuls of marshmallows.

"Thank you."

"Anything else you don't see that you want?" His eyes shifted from one side of the shop to the other before he looked at the floor.

"No, thank you," Sarah said, "I think I'm ready to pay you now." Sarah looked at all of the bushels, many of which were low on inventory, and at least half a dozen were empty. "Did you study chocolate making, too?" She handed her mesh bag filled with goodies to Maurice.

"No," he said, keeping his eyes fixed on the register as he rang up each item.

"Then how will you keep the store going?" Sarah asked.

"I'm figuring it out." His voice was gruff and dismissive. He told her the total and then ran her card.

Ginger was rung up next, and while Sarah waited for her, a guy Sarah had never seen before who would have looked at home on a Harley with a navy and white bandanna covering his bald skull; a thick leather jacket emblazoned on the back with a top rocker of DEMONS, a poison green and yellow flame patch, and a bottom rocker of IOWA; oil stained jeans; and black leather motorcycle boots walked through the door. He hung back and waited until Ginger's sale was finalized and she and Sarah were almost to the door before he approached the counter.

Ginger and Sarah got into the SUV but as she turned the key in the ignition, Sarah was watching drama unfold in the pop-up. The biker guy was gesturing with his arms out at his side, his hands making circles. Maurice was shaking his head no.

Sarah hit the button for her window to open. She knew it was a longshot but she wanted to see if she could hear them. Biker guy slammed his fist onto the table between him and Maurice with a "Don't tell me no!" And Maurice took a step backwards with his hands raised in front of him in a universal sign of surrender.

"I wonder what that's all about," Ginger said.

"No idea. But it doesn't look good. That guy looks pissed and not like someone I'd want to mess with."

"Me neither." Ginger reversed out of the space as Maurice and the biker dude went into the backroom.

Sarah pushed the button to raise her window.

CHAPTER TWENTY-ONE

After a busy Monday early morning with clients and telling Em all about her weekend adventures, at ten, Sarah took a break from Whiskey and the Coiffure to walk to the post office to see Cottageville Postmaster Luella Larkins, who was in her early fifties with short, curly, sandy hair and a bit of a cylindrical shape. She looked sharp in her pressed uniform but its gray hue washed out her complexion despite the rose lipstick she wore. She ushered Sarah into her office and as soon as she had the door closed, she said, "Chief James has been by. I'm so sorry to hear about the threats. They are very disturbing."

"Thank you. I brought a photo of the second envelope and message and of the address on the box delivered to my home in case your staff needs to know what the things looked like."

"Oh good. Thank you. Chief James did not bring photos."

Sarah showed her the pictures and then she emailed them to Luella, who promised to let all of her employees know and that they would be keeping their eyes open for any further letters, cards, or packages.

Luella shook her head. "I'm not sure how that package got through our scanning system. We x-ray things here."

"I don't think your machine looks for feces, does it? More like bombs and powders and things."

"That's true. I'm just sorry it got through, and I'm so glad you didn't open it." She wrinkled her nose and grimaced. "The thought of someone sending that... it's disgusting," Luella said, shaking her head again. "People can be so vile."

Sarah nodded, still unsettled by the memory of the package. "It's crazy that someone went out of their way to make me feel unsafe."

Luella's expression softened. "I can't imagine how that must feel. But you did the right thing by calling the police. We'll have to review our process, make sure this doesn't happen again." She sighed. "Unfortunately, there are always people looking to cause harm or discomfort in the most bizarre ways."

Sarah managed a weak smile. "At least it wasn't anything worse. Still, it's hard not to feel rattled." Then she thanked the postmaster for her time and for her assistance.

On her way back down Main Street, Sarah noticed the pop-up shop had a closed sign in the window but that the lights were on and

Maurice and two guys, who looked to be in their mid-forties, wearing dirty baseball caps from a farm equipment company, plaid flannel shirts, jeans, and boots were restocking the bushels and moving merchandise and displays around the store. Sarah paused for a second to try to understand what she was seeing, but then she realized they might see her so she scurried past.

Just as she passed their door, it opened and Maurice came out, carrying a box, which he put in the back of his mobile grooming van. He didn't seem to see her. The two guys followed him with boxes of their own which they also put in the van.

Sarah pretended to ignore what was going on behind her, as she turned onto her street, walked a few paces, and then leaned against the first building where she hoped she couldn't be seen. She peered from the shadows, curious if Maurice planned to close the pop-up early and leave town.

But he slammed the double doors on the back of the van after the three boxes, looked up and down Main Street, and then all three guys went back into his shop where they filled the bushels with candy. Then Maurice flipped the open sign on the door and the flannel wearers split, hoofing it south on Main Street.

Sarah returned to the Coiffure where Whiskey greeted her by stretching his front paws up her leg. She debated saying something to Emily about what she had spied at the candy store, but she didn't know what to make of it. Something just felt off, including the number of strangers that seemed to be in town lately. They looked a bit like what her grandmother used to refer to as "the rougher element," or men who were no strangers to bar fights or brawls.

Her phone chimed, jarring her from her thoughts. It was Jared saying he had decided to work a full day, until two, and that Ginger would take him home so Sarah didn't need to be his chauffeur this afternoon. She sent a thank-you text to Ginger and another to Jared saying she hoped his day was going well.

He sent back a red heart emoji in response.

"How was your sushi date with Travis?" Sarah asked Emily as she clipped the nails on a fourteen-pound black and tan Lhasa apso after its shampoo and trim.

"Fun. Turns out he's been doing Babbel Japanese so he tried to talk to the waiter, but the guy he was talking to was from Vietnam." Emily laughed. "He was so confident, too. He kept going, speaking what he thought was Japanese, and the waiter just looked so confused. Eventually, the poor guy was like, 'I don't speak Japanese, I'm from Vietnam,' and I thought I was going to die from secondhand embarrassment."

Sarah chuckled, shaking her head. "That's classic. He was trying so hard. But you know that saying about what happens when we assume."

"Exactly!" Emily said, still laughing. "I give him credit for the effort, though. He's been super dedicated to learning it. But yeah, wrong language, wrong person—he was mortified."

"At least he's trying to learn something new," Sarah said, smiling. "It's kind of endearing."

"Totally," Emily agreed. "We both laughed about it afterward. And hey, maybe next time he'll find someone who actually *speaks* Japanese."

"You didn't pull a second all-nighter?" Sarah clipped the last nail and then set the dog on the floor to visit with Whiskey.

"No way. I couldn't have even if I wanted to. It would have been way too much. We ate sushi, bought some candy canes from the pop-up shop—which was crazy-busy on Saturday night, by the way, with all kinds of people, mostly dudes I've never seen before—and then we ate the candy canes while walking through the park and playing on the swings, even though it was freaking cold out. But with the tree all lit and the stars out, it was kinda romantic." A bit of rosy color came to Emily's cheeks, which was something Sarah hadn't seen before.

"You like him." It wasn't a question.

Em looked down at the papillon on her stainless steel table, whose hair she was brushing. "I do."

"More than Taylor?" Sarah prodded with a question this time.

"Differently. With Taylor, we have fun and joke around and are stupid. We play-fight and..." Her voice trailed off as she gathered her thoughts. "He's like a brother I've never had or my BFF. It's awesome how well we get along. But with Travis, it feels like a date. It is still fun, but feels more serious. Not that I'm hanging out with a sibling or a friend. Does that make sense?"

"Totally."

"That's why I like spending time with both of them."

"Nothing wrong with that," Sarah said.

Hank opened the Coiffure's door and entered wearing his usual shorts, high socks, and black walking shoes. He wore a winter USPS jacket on his upper body making him look like he was straddling two opposing seasons. "Sarah. Emily. You are both looking fine today," he said as he set a stack of mail on the counter.

Sarah moved toward it as he added, "Luella texted all of us to be on the lookout for things from your mysterious sender. Sent photos, too. Nothing in that pile. I've already checked."

"Thank you so much, Hank," Sarah said, feeling tension seep from her body. She opened holiday cards, read them and shared some of the funnier canine humor ones with Emily, and then taped them around the window frame with the others.

Of course, she thought after Hank left, that didn't mean the mail that had been delivered to her home today was threat-free. But at least all missives in the Coiffure's delivery were positive and some were positively charming, or *pawsitively* charming in the case of one punny card.

Half an hour later, after the Lhasa apso had gone home, the Coiffure's green door opened again and in walked Candace Grimes in her police uniform. "Sarah," she said, "got a minute?"

Sarah met her in the waiting area, and they sat together on the chairs. Grimes held her phone out to Sarah so she could see the photo. A single piece of white paper with the black Sharpie block printing: YOU BETTER WATCH OUT. YOU BETTER NOT CRY. YOU BETTER NOT POUT. I'M TELLING YOU WHY. I'M COMING FOR YOU!!!

"That's what was in the box, separated by other papers, from the poop." Grimes pulled her phone back and put it into her jacket pocket.

"Wow. Can you, um, text that to me?"

"You really want this?" Grimes looked incredulous.

"I do so I can share it with Jared and have proof until the person is caught."

"Suit yourself. Just please, Sarah, keep yourself safe. Don't go anywhere alone. And call us if you see or hear or receive anything. I'm worried about you, my friend." Grimes put her hand on Sarah's and searched her eyes.

"Don't worry. I don't like this as much as you don't, and I'm taking it all very seriously." Then she let Candace know she had met with Luella and that Luella had already notified all of the Cottageville postal employees. "And Mrs. Jenkins and Robert and Bill are keeping an eye out for me and on my house too. And it looks like Jared isn't returning to his own place until all of this is behind us. "

"Those are all good things. We'll catch this person soon enough," Candace assured her. "I promise."

"I'm sure you will," Sarah said.

After Officer Grimes left, Sarah showed the photo to Emily, who said, "I can't believe this person is quoting a Christmas song as a threat. Who do they think they are? *Bad Santa*?"

"I think that role has already been taken by Billy Bob Thornton."

"It'd make more sense if they quoted The Police. 'Every Breath You Take' is stalker threat 101." Emily's emotions seemed to be getting the better of her.

Sarah walked toward her. "What's left on the butterfly dog?"

"A light trim and a bow."

"You want me to take over so you can take a break?"

"I should probably throw ice water on my face because right now my brain is trying to come up with menacing new lyrics to 'Silent

Night' and 'Jingle Bell Rock.' That's what the idiot has done to me."

"I get it. Here, let me trim the pup. What color bow are we doing?"

"Red. Thanks, Sarah." Emily went into the restroom and Sarah heard the water running. She sweet-talked to the little white and chestnut dog with the long, dropping fur around her stick up ears. The eight-pound bitch licked Sarah with her small pink tongue as she took just the ends off her fur so she would look more polished. As she was finishing, the Coiffure's front door opened and Whiskey ran to greet Tony and Spike, two of his favorite people. Tony was a monster-sized bodybuilder, who owned Big T's Fitness Center, and Spike was his seventy-five-pound pit bull, who looked just like his human.

Emily went into the waiting area to greet them as Spike and Whiskey rough-housed and chased one another under the counter, into the back, and around all of the grooming tables. "Whoa, slow down, guys," Emily called after them.

Tony put two fingers in his mouth and let loose a shrill whistle and the dogs skidded to a stop and stared up at him. "Much better. Sit. Both of you."

Their butts hit the floor in unison.

"Good boys," Tony said. "Em, can you give them treats?"

"Sure thing."

"Hey, Tony," Sarah called, setting the teeny dog on the counter as it seemed to be shaking because of Spike. Sarah knew he had a mushball heart inside his stocky and muscular physique but she didn't know how to relay that to the papillon.

"Yes, Sarah?" Tony wore white socks with black Adidas slides, black track pants, and a black Canada Goose jacket.

"Do you have self-defense classes at your gym?"

"Not really. You may want to talk to Kevin at the martial arts studio. That's more his thing. Are you interested generally or do you have an issue and need someone roughed up?" He chuckled at what he thought was a joke.

"Umm." Sarah hesitated, while Emily piped up, "Sarah, the whole town will know soon if they don't already. She's been receiving threats."

Emily got Spike to walk into a tub and Whiskey stayed nearby with his front paws on the lip of the tub and his face near his friend.

"What kind of threats?" Tony asked, his brows knitting together showing his concern.

"Mailed ones. Two came here, one in a Christmas card. Then on Saturday I got a package to my house. The police and fire departments came and did their thing to prove it wasn't a bomb."

"It was poop, if you can believe that," Emily let loose what sounded like a cackle.

"Umm, yep. She's right."

Tony didn't look any less worried. "What did the notes say?"

Sarah showed him the photos on her phone.

"Sarah, it sounds like you might need a bodyguard."

"I have Whiskey."

"He's awesome. But he has no professional protection training."

"That's true. All of the postal employees know and are on the lookout, the police keep doing drive-bys, my neighbors are all on alert. And I've not been going anywhere by myself..." Sarah frowned. "Except

I guess I did walk to the post office to meet with Luella and back by myself. That was probably a dumb move." She snuggled the papillon against her chest and the little dog licked her chin, which caused Sarah to grin.

"I know some guys that do personal protection work. I can make some calls if you want me to," Tony offered.

"I'll think about it. Did you want a holiday bandanna on Spike? He doesn't seem like the bow type."

"A bandanna is fine. Just nothing too cutesy. He has an image to uphold." Tony chuckled. "I'll be back in a couple of hours."

After he left, Sarah considered his suggestion of hiring a bodyguard until the police caught whomever was sending her the threats. She wasn't sure she'd like some stranger with her all of the time, and she already had Jared and Whiskey with her—one or the other or both—twenty-four-seven. Plus, so far everything had come through the mail system. It wasn't like she was being followed or had any threats through the phone or text or in person. She didn't even feel like someone was creeping around spying on her and watching her every move. When she really stopped to examine the past couple of weeks, it seemed like the sender wanted to trigger fear but was doing it from a distance. *Why would someone do it that way, if they really had it out for me?* Sarah wondered. But she couldn't come up with a concrete answer.

CHAPTER TWENTY-TWO

A half an hour after Sarah and Jared shared an evening comfort meal of homemade meatloaf, garlic mashed potatoes, and spicy sauteed green beans, snow lit up the night sky as it began to fall softly, casting a peaceful glow over the world outside. Sarah stood at the window with Whiskey at her side, watching the flakes dance in the light from the streetlamps. The snow seemed to quiet everything, offering a brief reprieve from the tension that had been swirling around them lately.

Jared joined her at the window, his crutches tapping lightly on the floor. "It's beautiful out there." His voice was low.

"Yeah," Sarah whispered, leaning her head against his shoulder.

"It almost makes everything feel Christmassy and normal."

"We need moments like this. It reminds me that not everything is drama-filled and dangerous, like parts of this month have been."

Sarah nodded, grateful for the small sense of peace. "You're right. It's nice to forget about everything else, even if it's just for a little while."

They stood there together, watching the snow blanket the world in white, the weight of the day momentarily lifted as they found comfort in the simple beauty of the night.

"It's a good night for hot chocolate," Jared said. "Would you like a mug with those big marshmallows you bought from Maurice?"

Sarah smacked her lips. "That's perfect for this snowy night. But why don't you relax and I'll go make it. You made our supper." She kissed his lips like a promise and wandered off to the kitchen to heat the oat milk, sugar, and cocoa. She grabbed two packages of marshmallows from the cupboard where she had stashed the candy. They were so fluffy, big, and square with textured pockets of air. Sarah stirred the cocoa mixture, ensuring it didn't scorch. When steam floated from the saucepan, she turned off the burner and poured half of the mixture into each mug. Then Sarah ripped open the cellophane packaging and pulled the two marshmallows out and plopped them atop one of the mugs. She reached for the second package of marshmallows when she realized a cellophane packet of something was sitting on the wax-coated paper in the bottom of the packaging.

Sarah picked up the packet and turned it forward and back in the kitchen lights. It was approximately two and a half inches square, flat, and contained a crystalline white powder. "What the heck..." she mumbled.

She tore into the second package of marshmallows, put those in the second mug of chocolate and then searched the rest of the packaging. No square packets of anything.

Sarah dumped all of the packages of marshmallows she had bought onto her kitchen counter, while raising her voice to make sure she was heard. "Jared, can you please come in here?"

While he maneuvered his way into the kitchen on his crutches, Sarah tore into the stash of marshmallows. Four packages were like the original ones she had bought. Six others contained the square packets of crystalline powder.

"What the heck is that?" Jared asked, eying the counter. He reached for one of the packets and Sarah said, "Don't touch it."

She whipped out her phone from her back pocket and dialed Ginger. When she answered on the first ring, Sarah asked, "Are you home?"

"Yes. We just finished eating. What's up? Did you see the snow?"

"Yes. I need you to open all of those packages of marshmallows you bought and tell me if anything besides marshmallows is in your packages. Pay special attention to the bottom of the packaging."

"Um, I'm not sure we want to eat a bunch of marshmallows. Like I said, we just ate."

"No, Ging, you have to do this. Please." Sarah snapped a photo of one of the packets and texted it to her BFF. "This is what was in six of mine. I need to know if they are in yours, too."

"What is that?"

Sarah could hear cellophane tearing in the background through Ginger's phone. "Holy crap, Sarah. I've got it, too."

"That's what I figured. I think the four of mine that are empty were the last ones in the bushel. My guess is he handed us ones from the wrong stash. I don't know what it is, but I'm betting it's illegal and maybe the shop was a front to deal drugs or anthrax or some kind of poison. Did you open them all yet?"

"Not quite but every single package has the white powder so far."

Sarah nodded her head even though Ginger couldn't see her. She motioned for Jared to call the police. He hobbled a few steps away from her and dialed.

"So, Jared is calling the police. Once they get through here, I'll have them go pick up the evidence at your place."

"Do you think we can eat at least a few of the marshmallows? They look and smell so good. Now I'm itching to make some hot chocolate and watch the snow."

"Probably not a good idea. I'd already made our chocolate and put in some of the marshmallows before noticing what was beneath them. They could be contaminated if the stuff leached."

"I can't believe you stumbled on another mystery or crime, Sarah. Way to go!" Affection from Ginger poured through the phone.

"It makes me wonder if what happened to Fiona is tied to this."

"Probably."

Jared said, "Officer Beams is still on the night shift so he said he'll be here soon."

"Did you hear that, Ginger?"

"I did. Thanks for calling. Let me know what he says. And Sarah, stay safe. I love you."

"I love you, too."

Sarah left everything on the counter, including the one hot chocolate with the marshmallows. She heated up another batch of the cocoa, sugar, and oat milk, but knew without the marshmallows it wouldn't be as good. Then, she and Jared stood near the window watching the snowflakes twirl and land and drinking their rich beverages while awaiting the police. Seven minutes later, John Beams pulled into Sarah's driveway. When she opened the front door, Whiskey greeted him first before trying to catch a snowflake in his mouth in the yard. The dog turned and jumped and acted like a piranha going after an insect. He was having a blast playing in the snowfall.

John smiled at Sarah and said, "We have to quit meeting like this."

"Believe me, I'd like nothing more. At least I received no threatening letters or suspicious packages today."

"That's good. But now you've gotten yourself mixed up in something else, maybe even something more sinister."

"Ginger, too. She bought marshmallows and chocolates when I did so I called her and had her open her marshmallows too. All of hers came from somewhere in the pop-up shop's backroom, but only ten of mine did."

"Wait. I'm going to need you to start at the beginning."

Sarah called Whiskey back into the house and shut the door and locked it, even though a cop car was in her driveway and an officer was in her house. She wasn't taking any chances. "Follow me," she said to John, leading him into her kitchen. She pointed to the counter where marshmallows lay like dead soldiers wherever they fell and the empty cellophane packaging reflected the overhead kitchen lights.

In his gloved hand Beams picked up one of the square packets and inspected it. "These have been popping up around town. We've had two OD deaths, one guy the Parks transported who made it, and we've busted a deal or two." John's eyes narrowed and his face hardened. "We couldn't trace it to a source. Weren't sure how it came to Cottageville."

"What is it?" Jared asked.

"Fentanyl. A few specks of it, like grains of salt, can kill a person. Hell, this packet right here has the potential to kill a dozen people."

"Oh no!" Sarah exclaimed.

"And the thing is," Beams continued, "it comes in way too many forms so you don't always know what you're looking for. We've seen it laced into club drugs, put into nasal spray and eye drops, or as liquid on blotter paper, in addition to these crystals and powder."

"I'm glad we stumbled upon it and Maurice screwed up my order because now you have somewhere to search. There has been an interesting trail of people in and out of there lately," Sarah uttered.

Beams nodded his head, pulled out his phone, and called Chief James. "Excuse me a minute," he said to Sarah and Jared and stepped into Sarah's living room. When he returned to her kitchen, he took photos of everything and then moved the cellophane outer wrappers and the packets into an evidence bag. "I'm taking the marshmallows on the counter too so they can be tested for traces of drugs. Nice work, Sarah. Thank you for helping us once again."

Sarah and Whiskey walked Officer Beams to the door, where she said, "And don't forget to send someone to Ginger's. She has evidence, too."

"We'll go get that tomorrow." He grinned, like he was thrilled with what he was about to say, "Tonight, we're headed to the candy store."

"Be safe," Sarah said, before locking the door again and turning the deadbolt.

As soon as he pulled out of her driveway, Sarah's phone rang. "Hello, Mrs. Jenkins."

"Sarah, I saw the police were at your house again. Are you okay? You didn't get another package, did you?"

"I'm fine. Thank you." For a split second Sarah wondered if she should tell Mrs. Jenkins what she found, but she realized gossip about the raid would be all over town before the sun rose tomorrow morning. News on the Cottageville grapevine traveled faster than the cars at the Indy 500.

When Sarah finished the story, Mrs. Jenkins said, "Even small towns aren't immune from the drug trade. There's too much money to be made in it. Just like in arms dealing and human trafficking."

Sarah wondered if arms dealing and human trafficking, too, had come to Cottageville, but she didn't want to ask and favored ignorance; she had enough to worry about right now. But she did file the question away in her memory to ask Mrs. Jenkins or Chief James on a different day. "I appreciate you keeping a watch out for me. The police haven't caught the person making threats to me. But I did talk to Luella today and her employees are on the lookout now, too."

"That's good news, dear. All of us working together will thwart the threat maker. I'm glad you are safe and well. Goodnight to you, Jared, and Whiskey."

"Thank you. Have a pleasant evening." Sarah disconnected and walked into the kitchen to find Jared loading their hot chocolate mugs into the dishwasher and then he washed down the kitchen counters, "Just in case those packets had holes in them," he said.

The snow continued to fall, carpeting the grass, the sidewalk, and the street in a layer of beautiful white. Sarah and Jared snuggled on the sofa, with Jared's leg on the coffee table for support and Whiskey curled into a ball beneath his best buddy. They binge watched a holiday themed baking show until Sarah felt idea overload for things she could make for her December 23 party, and they kept nodding off.

Finally, Sarah turned off the television and took Whiskey into the backyard for his final potty break of the night—what they referred to as his "last call". He romped into the snow that was barely an inch on the ground and flopped onto his back and wiggled into C's and reverse C's, just like he had weeks ago, making canine snow angels. When he popped back onto all fours, he grinned at Sarah, then he raced toward the back fence to pee.

A few hours later, Sarah was awoken from a deep and disturbing sleep. When she opened her eyes, she saw Whiskey standing atop her chest and he was nose to nose with her while Jared was rubbing her left arm. "What's going on?" she asked.

"You were screaming and shrieking. It woke me up and was terrifying." Jared parked his butt on the edge of her bed.

"I was? Actually, I was in my dream. Or I tried to but no sound was coming out. It was like they had scared the sound out of me. I couldn't do anything but open my mouth, which filled the air with silence."

"Scoot over, please," Jared said, stretching full length into the small strip of space between Sarah and the edge of her bed.

She moved over to give him more room and patted next to her for Whiskey to get off of her and to lay at her side. She became the filling in the Jared-Whiskey sandwich, and she didn't want to be anywhere else. Especially after the visions she had had.

"Tell me about your dream." Jared wrapped his arm around her and pulled her against him.

She took a deep breath and let it out before saying, "I was here in the house and a big—I mean big like Hulk Hogan size big—biker dude in a black leather vest over a black t-shirt smashed Fiona's head in with the sledgehammer and blood splattered all over my living room curtains. He came after me and Whiskey tried to fight him off, but he cracked Whiskey's skull with one swing of the hammer. I saw it and it felt like my heart stopped. I couldn't scream. I couldn't move. I couldn't save him. And I wasn't sure I cared if the man killed me, too. But instead of killing me or even chasing me, he made me watch while he went after everyone around me, one by one, taking them out with knives, swords, guns, hammers, all different kinds of weapons, but every weapon created so much blood. So much blood that it started to flood my house." Sarah paused. "I know that isn't rational."

"Nightmares rarely are. Did he kill me?"

"You, Ginger, Bill, Gladys, Candace, Emily, John, Chief James and Barbara, many people's pets. It was crazy. It was like he was killing everyone around me so I would be alone. So I would have no one." Sarah started to cry.

Jared held her tighter and kissed her hair.

"I didn't even know who the man was and why he was doing

what he was doing. I didn't want to watch it. I begged and pleaded with him to stop. I screamed at him. Or I tried to, but like I said, the sound wouldn't come out."

"Except it did. Because Whiskey and I heard you," Jared said against her hair. "And you're safe now. We have you. We're alive and well and you're with us. And we love you." It was the first time he had said it, and that made Sarah cry harder.

"I love you, too. Thank you. Thank you for being here with me and for keeping me safe."

She leaned over him to grab a tissue from her nightstand, blew her nose which was now stuffy from crying, tossed the tissue in the wastepaper basket next to the nightstand, and then snuggled back between her guys. "I'm sorry for waking you both. Let's try to get back to sleep."

Within minutes, they were, and Sarah was at peace.

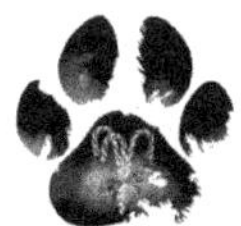

CHAPTER TWENTY-THREE

After dropping Jared off at work at six, Sarah and Whiskey went back home so she could shower and get ready for work. They had skipped their morning walk as Sarah was taking seriously the police directive to not go anywhere by herself, even if Whiskey was with her, but the lack of a morning walk irritated them both. Whiskey ran circles around the backyard and Sarah felt antsy.

At seven fifteen her phone rang, and when she answered, she heard Mrs. Jenkins say, "I'm going to be your walking buddy this morning. At least to Bill's. Is that okay with you? All of this snow is too pretty not to walk in."

"That's so nice of you." Sarah felt relief wash over her. "When would you like to leave?"

"We can go now, if you're ready."

"Let me get my boots, coat, scarf, and hat on and we'll meet you in front of your house."

"See you soon." Mrs. Jenkins disconnected.

"Come on, Whisk. We're walking with Mrs. Jenkins today."

Whiskey raced Sarah to the front door. She dressed for the cold and white weather, put her house keys and phone into her jacket pocket, and carried her empty to-go tumbler out the door, trailing behind Whiskey since she had to stop and lock up the house.

Mrs. Jenkins met Sarah at the sidewalk in front of her house. She had on a knit hat and lined leather gloves, a scarf wrapped around and around and around her neck and over her nose, and an almost to the ground wool coat.

"Love your coat," Sarah said.

"It's an old thing, but quality," Mrs. Jenkins said. Then she added in a low voice as she leaned toward Sarah, "And I like it because the pockets are deep so I can pack heat."

Sarah's eyes widened and she chuckled. "Good to know."

"Old habits die hard," Mrs. Jenkins said. "Now, Whiskey, you can run ahead, but remember I'm an old lady and can't walk as fast as you."

He smiled up at her, before running five feet ahead to pee on a snow-covered rhododendron. "So, you're going to Bill's this morning?" Sarah asked.

"Sure. He'll give me some coffee and maybe we'll have breakfast. It was more an excuse so you wouldn't try to go anywhere by yourself, honestly. We're all worried about you. And we know your routine. Walk Whiskey. Stop at Bill's. Get coffee, pastries, and salads at Java and Juice. Walk to the Coiffure. Work. Walk home through the park. We all talked about and knew that if we know your routine and where you are at many points of the day the person who sent those things to you may know, too. You, and all of us, are creatures of habit."

Sarah pursed her lips. She hadn't thought about her life in that way or that she could be easily found or ambushed because of her habits. "I appreciate you all looking out for me, and I'm grateful you were willing to brave the cold and snow with me this morning."

"This is nothing, honey. I lived in the Alps for a spell and in the Nordic countries. Finland, in particular, will chill you in a way you'd think it would take months for your bones to thaw." Mrs. Jenkins' face eased into a knowing smile.

They traveled Sarah's usual route through the park, which was completely deserted this morning. The snow was unblemished, not a footprint from human or animal anywhere on the soft, white surface, until Whiskey trotted through and then circled back to them. While his breed may have been used to the desert conditions of the Outback, Whiskey considered himself a snow bunny, whooshing every which way through the powder, causing Sarah and Janice to laugh more than once.

When they reached Bill's house, Sarah was surprised to see him bundled in a parka and sitting on his porch, the newspaper spread in front of him, a cup of coffee sending swirls of steam into the atmosphere to his right. "Good morning, ladies, Whiskey." He pulled a chicken flavored biscuit from his ever-present jar of dog treats and handed it to Whiskey.

"Good morning, Bill," Sarah said, while Janice stood next to him. "Mind if I go in and pour myself a cup?" Jancie asked.

"Not at all. Sarah?"

She held up her tumbler and said they were on their way to Java and Juice and then to work.

"Want me to walk you?" Bill asked, his eyes shooting up over his glasses.

"No. It's only a few blocks. I'll be okay."

"Well, I'm going to stand on the sidewalk here and watch you go to Java and Juice." He got up from the table and came down the steps. "The chief would have my head if something happened to you from my house to there."

"Okay. Thank you," Sarah said. She and Whiskey crossed the street, which was easy since no traffic was on Main Street, and walked the one block to Java and Juice and opened the bright red door. Whiskey entered and Sarah waved to Bill and Janice before she shut the cafe's door.

Jared was at the register and his face punctuated with a grin when he saw them. No one was in line and only Barbara Order and Mayor Trish took up space at the table furthest from the door. Barbara was in her usual weekday attire of yoga tights but she had thrown a long-sleeve shirt over her fitted coordinated-with-her-tights tank top. Mayor Trish wore boots under a wool skirt, blouse, and blazer. The coats of both women were thrown over the empty chair at their table.

"Greetings, Sarah. I heard you had quite the surprise in your sweets last night." Barbara's face broke into a smile.

"Did Chief James pull another all-nighter?" Sarah asked, before handing Jared her cup and telling him she wanted two of the candy cane chocolate chunk scones and two barbeque chicken salads. "Oh, and maybe two of those cinnamon cream eclairs."

"It wasn't as late as the other night," Barbara said.

"Sarah, you sure deserved that Citizen of the Year award," the mayor said. "You've done a lot to keep us safer."

"Some of it just by chance," Sarah mumbled, tapping her credit card against the reader and taking the bag from Jared. "See you later, roomie." She smirked and then leaned across and planted a soft kiss on his lips.

"Awww," Ginger said. She had come out of the backroom with a tray of freshly baked mini-pies. Sarah couldn't tell what the flavors were but they smelled like cinnamon, brown sugar, and deliciousness.

"Want me to ring up two of those?" Jared asked.

"Umm, no, thank you. But if there's any left at the end of your shift, maybe you could bring two home to go with our dinner."

Ginger chuckled. "Talk to you later, Sarah."

"Bye. And have a good day, everyone."

Just as she and Whiskey were poised to walk out the door, Barbara and Trish whooshed to her side. They pulled on their coats. "Not so fast," Barbara said. "We're walking you to the Coiffure. Jimmy made it very clear to me that if I saw you out and about and no one was with you I was to stick with you until you reached your destination."

"Ahh, okay," Sarah said, realizing she didn't have a choice. Whiskey took the lead, followed by Sarah and the mayor walking side by side with Barbara bringing up the rear for the two blocks south on

Main Street. They paused at the closed candy shop, with its police tape, and disarray. An officer stood in the front, guarding the place, and he tipped his hat to the mayor and the chief's wife.

They waited for a white Subaru Outback and a black Ford F-150 to pass before they crossed Main Street and walked the block to Sarah's Coiffure. Sarah put her keys in the lock and opened the door and flipped on the lights. Whiskey trotted in ahead of them and waited for them to enter. Once Barbara and Trish were certain there was no one lurking inside waiting to attack Sarah, they bid her a good day and saw themselves out. She locked the door behind them.

"Is this really how it's going to be, boy?"

In response, Whiskey gave a little whine and swiped her shin with his paw. His brown eyes gazed up at her with love.

Sarah put the pastries on the table and the salads in the fridge, then she hung her winter jacket and donned her denim apron. She topped off the shampoo bottles and set a stack of towels at each of the stations, after looking over the schedule to see which animals were coming to the Coiffure today and for what service.

Emily arrived and Whiskey flew to the front room to greet her. As Em was shutting and locking the door behind her, she was already talking. "Did you see it, Sarah? The pop-up shop was raided by the police last night, and Maurice and two other guys were taken away in handcuffs. It was so cool. Somebody live streamed it. Sascha was part of the action, straining on her leash, sniffing the ground, with the chief trying to restrain her."

"Sascha was there? I didn't think the chief took her to work."

Emily hung up her jacket and threw the denim apron over her

black sweater and black jeans. Her black leather Doc Marten boots had a dusting of snow on the toes. "Hang on a sec, and I'll pull up the video on my phone. It's on the neighborhood page." Emily put her bag away and set her peppermint latte on the table before sliding her phone from the back pocket of her jeans."

Sarah watched in awe as the police, in tactical gear and looking like a SWAT team—instead of her neighbors and friends—ran through the front door of the candy store with the voice of someone yelling, "Go, go, go. Hands up. Get them in the air" providing the soundtrack. And sure enough Sascha and Chief James brought up the rear behind the other officers.

"There's video of the alleyway too and police busting in through there," Emily said. "But I think those guys were from the county, as one of their vests said so."

"That makes sense that the Cottageville Police would need the extra help. We aren't a big town and don't have many officers."

"Well, I think they all got called in for this." Emily pulled up another video of an officer protecting Maurice's head as he got into the back of the police cruiser, his hands cuffed behind him." A second video showed the biker dude and some guy Sarah had never seen being shoved into other police cars.

"Isn't it insane? Right here in our sleepy little town." Emily bit into her eclair and closed her eyes, clearly loving the pastry. "I don't know why they were raided but—"

Sarah interrupted. "I do." Then she told her about the marshmallows.

"So, you tipped off the police? Nice detective work, Sarah."

"No, no detective work. I think it was a mistake on Maurice's part. One I'm sure he's regretting." She wondered about him and what his and Fiona's story was. She barely knew him, but she could tell how devastated he was by what happened to Fiona. She was sure he hadn't faked his grief.

Emily and Sarah ate their pastries and drank their coffee in silence before Sarah unlocked the door, signaling she was ready for business. As clients trickled in all day wanting their pets pampered and prepped for the holidays, few talked about anything else but the raid. Rumors flew claiming the police found everything from child porn to cocaine, that they busted up a dog napping ring and arrested a bunch of wanted outlaws. Sarah was surprised and amused at the stories people created or believed. Very few of her neighbors and clients knew the truth that there was fentanyl in the marshmallows, and Sarah and Emily corrected no one. It wasn't their place, and Sarah admitted to herself that even she didn't know the whole story. She hadn't been a part of the raid and she didn't know what the police found or didn't.

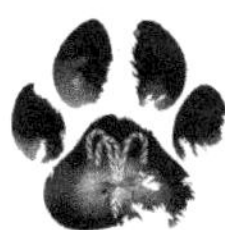

CHAPTER TWENTY-FOUR

At five, as Sarah and Emily were sweeping the floors, putting the towels in the washer, and generally cleaning up after a busy day, the Coiffure's front door opened and Officer Beams walked in and locked the door behind himself. Whiskey ran to greet him and got two handed scratches on his head, ears, and back, which caused him to lean into John's leg, with a silent message of "Don't stop. Don't stop."

John's eyes looked sunken, and his under eyes looked bruised like he hadn't had much sleep. "Chief James asked me to stop by and thank you for helping us figure out part of the supply chain of the drugs."

"I'd like to think I'd do what any Cottageville citizen would do if they found fentanyl in their packages of marshmallows." Sarah grinned.

"It was more than that. This was part of a pretty nasty ring running drugs in half a dozen, maybe more, states."

"Oh wow," Emily said. "And your raid is all over the internet. I hope that doesn't put targets on your backs." Then she covered her mouth with her fingers like she just realized the implications of what had flown out of it.

"Yeah. Me, too." John rubbed a hand over his face.

"Is Maurice...um..." Sarah wasn't sure how to ask what she wanted to know.

"Maurice was in over his head. He had been trying to get out. But the guys at the top thought the mobile grooming and pop-up chocolate shops were the perfect cover. They pulled the strings and sent them where they needed them. When Maurice and Fiona wanted to back away, well, they attacked Fiona as a warning to Moe."

"Oh my gosh." Tears pooled in Sarah's eyes.

"It's sad. The whole story rushed out of him last night. He seemed almost relieved. Like we had saved him from the charade he no longer wanted to play."

"What will happen to him?" Sarah asked.

"I don't know. That's up to the judge and the D.A. Anyway, I thought you deserved to know what happened since you found Fiona and the fentanyl. There were a few other drugs hidden, too. Sascha found them."

'She did?" Sarah asked, impressed.

"Yes. She may look like the Orders' family pet, but she's actually had extensive training as a drug dog. We just need to use her so rarely around here.”

“You hear that, Whiskey? Sascha has a job.”

He flashed her a black gummed smile.

“Anyway, I need to be on my way. And Sarah, Maurice said he’s had nothing to do with your threats, and I believe he’s telling the truth. So please keep up the buddy system and locking those doors until we get some closure on who sent you the letters and package. You didn’t get anything today, did you?”

“Not here. Not sure about at home.”

“Okay, call if you receive anything.” The microphone and speaker on his shoulder squawked about a car stuck in a ditch. “Gotta go. Have a nice night.”

“You, too,” Sarah said.

“Bye,” Emily said. “I’m gonna drive you and Whiskey home because you heard the man.”

“Sounds good.” Sarah took off her apron, put on her jacket, and said, “Time to go, Whisk,” before locking up and getting into Emily’s car. The snow no longer covered the street, having melted in the afternoon sun, at least on the main streets. On Sarah’s residential street a dusting still blew around as the Honda moved the air.

“Have a drama-free night,” Em said as she pulled into Sarah’s driveway.

“I’d love one. Thank you, Em. Come on, Whiskey, let’s go see Jared.” She waved to her assistant and walked to her front door. While she used the key on both locks, Whiskey took a pitstop to water an azalea. He raced to the kitchen where the most tantalizing smells were wafting from the room.

"It smells like homemade bread and some kind of tomato-based sauce." Sarah ditched her shoes into the front closet and hung her jacket on the rack.

"That's because I've made sauce and pizza." Jared's back was to her as he plated lettuce leaves and topped them with halved cherry tomatoes, sliced cucumbers, and disked carrots.

"Are you sure you need to work and can't just be my personal chef?" Sarah wrapped her arms around him from behind. "Though with all of these amazing meals, I may gain a pound or two."

He turned around in her arms and said, "No matter. You'll always be mi'lady," and he kissed the tip of her nose.

"Do I have time for a quick shower?"

"You have seven minutes," he said.

"Precise." She jogged toward her bedroom.

Five minutes later she was back in the kitchen. Whiskey had been fed, and she was picking up the plates, utensils, hot chili flakes, extra parmesan, and the salads and carrying them into the dining room. She asked Jared if he wanted wine, beer, water, or anything else with his meal.

"Maybe later," he said. "Hey, have you been online today?"

"You mean have I seen the videos? Emily was so pumped up when she came into work. She couldn't stop talking about them."

"Same with everyone who came into Java and Juice."

Jared removed the pizza from the oven. Green dots of basil punctuated the light yellow of the mozzarella and rings of bell peppers circled mushrooms and pepperoni. "Those are turkey pepperonis," he explained. "I like them because they aren't as greasy."

"The whole pizza is like a work of art."

He wheeled the pizza cutter through the crust creating perfect triangles, before asking Sarah if she could carry it for him into the dining room.

As they ate, Sarah told him about Officer Beams' end of day visit. "Oh that reminds me," Sarah said. "Did I get any mail today?" Her heart sank as she asked and her stress levels skyrocketed. She really, really dreaded getting any more letters, packages, or threats.

"What looks like some Christmas cards and a bill or two, plus some junk flyers. I flipped through—I hope you don't mind—but I didn't see anything with that telltale black Sharpie or block printing."

Sarah whooshed out an audible breath. "Oh, thank God."

As Sarah picked up a second slice of pizza and took a bite, her doorbell rang, sending Whiskey into a frenzy of barking and running. He was going so fast on the hardwood floors that he slid into the front door but that didn't stop his barking.

Sarah stood up and walked through the door, looking through the peephole. "It's the chief," she said to Jared.

She opened the door. "Hey, Chief James. Want some pizza? It's homemade. Jared really outdid himself."

"Evening, Sarah. I'd love a slice, but this isn't a social call." He stood in the doorway.

"Come in. Come in." Sarah stood back and shooed Whiskey aside so Chief James could enter their house. "Want to give me your coat?"

"Nah, I don't know how long I'll be staying."

"You sure you don't want some pizza?" Sarah watched the chief hesitate before he said, "Well one slice won't hurt. It smells delicious."

"Here, let me hang up your coat and go in with Jared. I'll get you a plate."

When Sarah was back at the table, she asked, "So what brings you here tonight?"

"It's about your package sender." The chief paused and took a bite of his food. "This is really good, Jared." He chewed thoughtfully, then swallowed, and put the slice back on his plate, turning his focus to Sarah.

"Luella's people intercepted a package on its way to you this afternoon."

Sarah's eyes widened. "And?"

"It was more of the same." Chief James' voice relayed his disappointment and did nothing to hide his anger.

"Do you know who sent it?" Jared asked, looking from the chief to Sarah.

"Yes. It was sent from the jail."

"What?!" Sarah couldn't believe what she just heard.

"That's pretty ballsy for someone to send threats from there. How'd it get past security? Isn't mail monitored?" Jared asked, throwing his napkin onto his plate like he was disgusted.

"Yes. So we are looking into that."

"Who? Who's in jail and hates me?" Sarah asked, creases forming between her brows.

Chief James leaned toward Sarah and whispered the answer.

"Wow. Just wow. Glad he's taking responsibility for his actions." Sarcasm dripped from Sarah's words as she crossed her arms, trying to process the absurdity of the situation. "So, let me get this straight: He's sending me threats from *jail* because this year I saved the people he almost destroyed? Unbelievable." And figuring out that mystery was part of the reason she had been honored as Citizen of the Year. *No wonder this started when that happened,* Sarah thought.

Chief James nodded solemnly. "I know it sounds crazy, but some people hold onto grudges like that, even when they're the ones in the wrong. We're taking this very seriously, though, Sarah. We're tracing every step of how that package and those letters got through, and we'll make sure he faces additional charges for this."

Jared clenched his jaw. "I just don't get it. How can someone be that twisted? Instead of reflecting on his actions, he's blaming *her*."

"It's all about control," Chief James said. "After all he had planned for years, he lost control of the situation, and now this is his way of trying to get some of that control back. But we won't let him succeed."

Sarah shook her head, still incredulous. "It's so messed up. I was just doing what anyone would have done."

"Well, not everyone," Chief James said with a slight smile. "You did something brave, and you saved lives."

"You know the best part of this discovery?" Jared asked, looking at Sarah.

She said nothing, waiting for him to continue.

"The dude is in jail on attempted murder charges and one count of attempted manslaughter. He's awaiting trial and didn't make bail. He may have been saying he was coming to get you, but he can't. There's no physical way for him to do that. From him, you're perfectly safe. What you've seen is the only way he could have lashed out."

"He's right. There's no reason for you to be looking over your shoulder any more. And he'll never send you another threat. We'll make sure of it."

"Wow. It's over," Sarah said, her eyes filling with tears of relief. "Did you hear that, Whiskey? We can take our normal morning walks and we won't need chaperones. It's a Christmas miracle."

Chief James and Jared chuckled at Sarah's comment. The chief finished his piece of pizza, complimented Jared one more time, and thanked Sarah for her help this month. Before he left, Sarah said, "If you, Barbara, and Sascha are free, I'm holding a holiday open house on December 23. Feel free to come by and celebrate with us."

"That sounds wonderful, Sarah. Thank you."

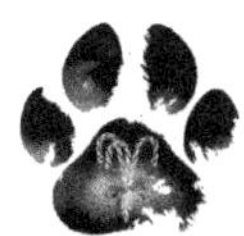

CHAPTER TWENTY-FIVE

The following week, Jared was still wearing the cast, but he was hopping around better without the crutches as his leg no longer hurt when he put weight on it. But he was counting down the days until the cast was scheduled to come off in mid-January. He couldn't wait. He started back at Java and Juice working full days, but he was still stuck on his stool and at the register. Because of the holidays and everyone out and about, the cafe was doing a record amount of business each day. Since he wasn't permitted to drive, Sarah continued to drop him off at work in the mornings and either Taylor or Ginger drove him back to Sarah's house. But she, herself, walked to work each day with Whiskey by her side, greeting her friends and neighbors, and relishing the return to normal. No more looking over her shoulder or wondering who was out to get her.

The storefront of the pop-up candy shop had been fully processed by law enforcement and now stood vacant, awaiting a new tenant in the new year. Every day when Sarah passed the space she felt sadness and loss, for Fiona, whom she never knew, for the fabulous chocolate and the best marshmallows she had ever eaten, and for mistakes humans made from which some of them never recovered. She wished that whatever business went in there next would benefit the community, not cause it harm. She even mumbled that as a kind of mantra every morning on her way to her business.

By December 22, the Coiffure had sold out of all of their holiday accessories so she and Em moved the four-way display rack into a storage closet to save it for next time, though Emily tried to coax Sarah into keeping it up all year and selling seasonal merchandise, like heart bandannas and red rhinestone collars for Valentine's Day and rabbit ears for dogs for Easter. Sarah wasn't sure she wanted to delve too deeply into the merchandise game, content to provide a service instead of products, which required an upfront investment greater than that of their services.

Sarah was washing Pedro the great Pyrenees, while his elfin size human Kristen Powers, impeccably dressed in a cashmere sweater and wool dress pants, sat in the Coiffure's waiting area, making phone calls to her real estate clients. Pedro shook his drenched whitish fur as Sarah rinsed him. "Ugh!" she exclaimed as strings of water flew from the dog all over Sarah, Emily, and Whiskey—who was near the tub providing moral support. Then Sarah and Em busted out laughing.

"I'm so glad we can have fun as we work," Emily said. "I listen to the stories from Travis, and Sergio makes everything so serious."

"I'm glad too, Em. And you didn't tell me, who are you bringing to my party tomorrow night? Travis or Taylor?"

"Both." Emily wiggled her eyebrows and giggled. "Travis is my date, but Taylor likes you and Jared so he's coming, too. The three of us get along just fine."

"Oh that's good news."

"What should we bring?"

"Your holiday cheer. We've got the rest of it covered." Sarah smiled to herself. She couldn't wait to give Emily her Christmas gifts. She put together a bunch of things: a black t-shirt emblazoned with "'I BRUSH YOUR DOG" in big letters and "I won't have to shave them. It's not that complicated" in small letters, which she knew would crack Em up; plus another black t-shirt with the words "Your Dog Isn't Going to Brush Itself" in white on the chest; a candle that said "Smells Like the World's Best Dog Groomer" on the front of glass jar; and a sterling silver dog paw on a chain. She wanted Emily to feel how much she appreciated her, not just for her skilled work and patience with the pets and their humans, but also for her friendship.

They tag-teamed the blow drying, trimming, and styling of Pedro as he was massive and well over one hundred fifty pounds. When they were guiding him from the tub, he reared onto his hind legs for a stretch and the gentle giant almost towered over five-foot-six Sarah. Kristen commanded from her spot on the sofa, "Pedro, down," and the dog complied.

Forty-five minutes later, Pedro left the Coiffure sporting a silky coat and a big shiny gold bow around his neck. He looked Christmas card worthy, and Kristen expressed her gratitude for helping make her boy more handsome. She gave both Sarah and Emily large tips as holiday thank-you presents.

When Sarah and Whiskey got home from work that night she found three candy cane poinsettias on her kitchen counter. "Officer Grimes dropped those off and said they were compliments of the police department. And Ginger sent three cheesecakes, eggnog, chocolate with peppermint, and a bourbon pecan one for tomorrow night. She said to let her know if you need anything else."

"That's incredible,' Sarah said.

"I made a sheet pan of chicken breasts and roasted root vegetables for supper," Jared said. "I know we have a lot of work to do tonight for tomorrow's party so I chose something easy that didn't use a lot of cookware."

"You're so thoughtful," Sarah said, giving him a hug. "Thank you for taking care of me when I'm supposed to be taking care of you."

"It's a two-way street. That's what makes a partnership work." Jared pressed his lips against hers and brushed some stray ginger hairs from her face. "If you set the table, I'll pull this from the oven."

"It's a deal," Sarah said.

As they ate, they went through the list of what they needed to do tonight and what was on their agendas tomorrow, as they both had taken the day off. They would split the cooking, and Sarah wanted to finish some decorations, like adding the three new poinsettias to a holiday display she had started on her porch. She had originally planned the party to be small and low-key, but as she thought about how many people had helped her over the last year and even over the last month, how they had looked out for her and had cared about Jared in his recovery, she wanted to spend time with each and every one of them. So the guest list grew and grew, and Sarah wasn't even sure how many people would stop by but that was okay with her. All of Cottageville was welcome, pets included.

And this would be the first holiday that she and Jared would celebrate as a couple, the first party they were throwing together, and that warmed her heart. It felt like a turning point, not just in their relationship but in her life. After everything they'd been through—the threats, the fear, and the uncertainty—this holiday party was a celebration of resilience, love, and community.

"I'm really looking forward to tomorrow," Sarah said, smiling at the thought of their growing guest list. "It's going to be chaotic, but in the best way."

She beamed with joy as they continued planning the night's tasks, listing last-minute groceries and decorations, with Jared occasionally teasing her about going overboard with the festive details. But she didn't mind. This wasn't just any party—it was a testament to how far they'd come, and how much they had to celebrate.

And when the evening of December 23 arrived, Sarah greeted her guests while wearing her fun, red and white Nordic-style *Happy Howlidays* sweater that featured three cattle dogs across the front, which she paired with black velvet leggings and black booties. Jared proudly wore a dark green sweater Sarah had custom made with Whiskey's face on the front and the words *Whiskey's Best Bud*. It wasn't ideal with his gray sweatpants, but he still couldn't get a pant leg over his cast, and fashion was the least of his concerns anyway. He sat on the sofa in Sarah's living room, his healing leg resting with his foot on the coffee table. Whiskey and Sascha lay under his leg, with Maple close by and keeping an eye on them. His nose wiggled with the scents of dogs, food, and fragrances worn by many of the guests. The front door opened and Gladys, Janice, and Bill, along with Kahlo and Cassatt, came in. Bill took two wrapped packages from the women and placed those under Sarah's tree, while Sarah took their coats. She hugged them one by one, and fussed over the poodles in their festive sweaters. Bill handed Sarah a wine bag and said, "That's for you, not for the party," before he kissed her cheek.

"Thank you," she said as she led them into the house, and pointed out where the food and drinks were available for self-serving. "Let me know if you need anything else. I can make tea, hot chocolate, and coffee." They picked up plates and added shrimps with cocktail sauce; mini quiches; charcuterie items such as meats, cheeses, nuts, and dried fruits; Swedish meatballs; mushroom toasts; spinach and artichoke dip; bacon-wrapped cheese stuffed dates; and much more onto their plates.

Sarah's eyes got misty as she glanced around her home and saw all of the people she loved. Her heart felt such peace as laughter and chatter rose above the Christmas music. She decided right there and then that she needed to say something. She grabbed a champagne glass, added some bubbly, and grabbed a fork to tap against it. She raised her voice, "Excuse me. Excuse me, everyone."

A hush went through the crowd.

"Stand up on the coffee table, Sarah," Jared said. "That way everyone can see and hear you."

She slipped off her booties and climbed on to the wood table in her stocking feet. "Thank you all for celebrating the holidays with me. I'm so amazed to see so many of you here." She nodded towards Chief James and Barbara, John Beams and Braidington Bradley, Mayor Trish, Ginger and Daniel, Daisy and Donovan, Daphne Smith, Emily and her guys, and dozens of people who meant so much to her and who had impacted her life. "We've been through so much together this year, and in these last few weeks in particular. And in some ways, I think the trials we've faced have made us come together better as a community. My grandmother loved this town. When she moved here all those many years ago, she said she had finally found the home she didn't know her heart had been missing." Sarah wiped a tear from her eye. She missed Gigi. "I never knew what she meant until recently. Though I have parents and a brother, you've all become my family. And not even a dysfunctional one," Sarah joked.

"Are you sure about that?" Chief James asked. "In my role, it sometimes looks that way."

Everyone laughed.

"I guess what I'm trying to say is I'm so glad I live here in Cottageville and count you all as my neighbors and friends. You're all the best and I love you. To all of us." Sarah raised her glass. "May we always care for each other and look out for each other, and well, though it sounds hokey, be for each other the love we wish to see in the world. At Christmas time and always."

"Cheers," Mayor Trish yelled. "To the best damn town and its people."

A laugh rippled through the crowd, and Whiskey barked twice, which caused all of the other dogs present to join in.

Maple took off running to the nearest corner, as the barks were beyond his comfort zone, and Candace Grimes was hot on his tail to soothe him.

Jared pushed himself off the sofa and hobbled over to Sarah. He wrapped his arms around her and said into her ear. "Best party ever. I'm so glad we are together. I love you. Merry Christmas, mi'lady. I look forward to many more."

THE END

Want more Whiskey the Cattle Dog Mysteries? Read a sneak preview of book four in the series, *Paws, Promises, and Peril*, which will be released on February 1. To sign up to receive sneak previews and release dates about other books in the Whiskey Dog Mystery Series, go to https://www.whiskeydogmysteries.com

PAWS, PROMISES, AND PERIL

WHISKEY DOG MYSTERY #4

CHAPTER 1

"Why did I ever decide to oversee the annual Valentine's Day Pet Parade and festivities?" Sarah Carter asked herself for the hundredth time. Sure, it had seemed like a fun idea last month when a canine in a cupid costume crossed her social media feed and caused her and her assistant, Emily Colt, to chuckle and wish that their town had a parade of pets. But now that the event was fourteen days away, and her grooming salon, Carter's Canine Coiffure, was slammed with appointments before the big day—plus she was still navigating the permits, vendors, and logistics not to mention the pet parents who demanded more attention and control than the worst bridezillas—Sarah wondered if her amusing brainstorm with Em was turning into a nightmare.

Cottageville, a small town in Iowa, had its share of characters and animal lovers, or maybe the animal obsessed was more like it. The parade was turning into a huge to-do, with more than one hundred pets registered to march. And it wasn't only the pawed and canine variety. Em's friend Taylor signed up Iggy the iguana to crawl down Main Street. Five people planned to walk cats on leashes—which with some cats was as effective as trying to herd them. Pat from Cottageville Animal Rescue was bringing a whole menagerie for which she needed to find foster and permanent homes, including a bow-wearing descented skunk named Petunia. And just yesterday, Sarah received a call from a guy asking if his blue and red tarantula could take part in the parade. She wasn't sure how any of this would work out. Even her Australian red heeler cattle dog, Whiskey, who loved almost every human and most critters, was suspicious of the skunk, and she had no idea how he'd respond to an arachnid.

And when you combined the wearing of costumes—which triggered reluctance and feelings of insecurity in some of furred and feathered set—with species who have been stereotyped sworn enemies for a reason, those cats and dogs, rabbits and skunks, snakes and spiders, hamsters and guinea pigs, and the lizard or two, could cause things to go very wrong very quickly. If one animal felt threatened or a lack of confidence, chaos could ensue.

Sarah felt her heart rate increase and her anxiety spike just thinking about it. She intentionally took some deep cleansing breaths and sighed them out, willing in some calm and inner wisdom. She told herself, "You've got this," but the words sounded hollow, even in her head. Instead, she focused on what was in front of her: the park and its expansive sparkling ice crystal designs. She gazed at the top bar of the swing set and the side of the slides, which sported icicle drips. Mandala patterns bloomed in ice lace between the climbing ropes on the north end of the jungle gym. Winter bloomed in all of her beauty, with Mother Nature as artist extraordinaire.

Sarah zipped her navy-blue puffy jacket to ward off the February chill and scrunched her neck into the jacket's collar, like a turtle shrinking into its shell. She should have put a knit beanie on top of her damp auburn hair before she left the house. But she was in a hurry. On days like this, when the wind was whipping, she envied Whiskey, with his double coat of fur. He was off-leash as usual and ahead of her, following his nose along the dusting of snow gracing the grass like powdered sugar atop a chocolate crinkle cookie. The park was empty at six-thirty on a weekday, which was the way Sarah liked it since it was usually her thinking time. But right now, thinking was the last thing she needed to do.

So, she watched Whiskey on his sniff fest and wondered what had been through the park before them. A raccoon or opossum, possibly? Or had it been one of his friends, like Sascha the German shepherd, and his human police chief James Order? Whiskey's interest seemed intrigued, not agitated, as he followed a trail invisible to Sarah's eyes. He eventually led her out of the park and to the front porch of Bill, an elderly widower who was popular with the gray-haired grannies, and who sat outside with his morning coffee and newspaper every day of the year, regardless of the temperature. Next to Bill was the target of Whiskey's mission to visit: a gallon jar of dog treats.

"Top of the morning to you, Whiskey, Sarah," Bill greeted, reaching into the jar of treats. He wore a trapper hat with the flaps up, an old quilted flannel jacket buttoned over what looked to Sarah like a gray sweatshirt and jeans that may have been flannel lined, and wintry sheep's fleece lined slippers over his socks. He asked Whiskey to slap him five, and once the dog's right paw hit Bill's palm, he handed Whiskey the biscuit. "How are you today?" Bill's eyes met Sarah's.

"I'm okay. Stressing a little over the parade and Valentine's Day festivities," she admitted.

"The guys at the hall asked if you needed help with security or route set-up, check-in, or anything else. We're available the day of or to help with anything you need before or after, including clean-up." Though Bill had never been a farmer, he had joined the Grange Hall years ago for companionship after his wife had died.

"Wow. That's so generous of you. I would love some help. I think Janice Jenkins said she'd work the check-in table, but she could probably use an assistant and I could use help with set-up, security, and clean-up, for sure. Do you want me to create a sign-up sheet for you to take to the hall, or should anyone who wants to volunteer just contact me?" Janice Jenkins lived across the street from Sarah, and she and Bill were close friends, maybe more.

"You have enough on your plate, Sarah. I can be the point person and coordinate all of the positions and people. Just let me know what jobs you need to have filled. I'm happy to help and have plenty of time." Bill took a sip of his coffee.

"I can't thank you enough." Sarah leaned down and gave him a side hug. "I'll send you an e-mail with the details. Come on, Whiskey, we've got to get going. Thanks again, Bill."

Sarah took off at a jog back through the still-empty park, with Whiskey running alongside her. The overwhelm she had been feeling for days had been carried away like a helium balloon, thanks to Bill and his Grange Hall friends.

When they returned to the craftsman bungalow that Sarah had inherited almost seven years before from her grandmother, Gigi, she fed Whiskey his breakfast, which he gobbled down in what seemed like a breath. Then, before she forgot, Sarah pulled out the folder for the pet parade and typed up the email to Bill on the various volunteer positions that needed to be assigned. She reiterated how grateful she was for their willingness to help. And she offered to take Bill out to dinner to thank him once the festivities were over.

Sarah grabbed her to-go tumbler, slid her feet into boots and her arms into the sleeves of her jacket. She added her scarf and beanie to the ensemble this time, before she zipped her jacket, and then she and Whiskey locked the door to their home and walked back toward the park to go to work. As they approached the children's playground, Sarah spotted Gigi's best friend and the woman who had become an adopted grandmother to her, Gladys Rossmiller, and her miniature poodles, Kahlo and Cassatt, who were sniffing below the swings. Gladys was wrapped in a long royal blue coat, with a lavender scarf wrapped and wrapped and wrapped around her eighty-year-old neck. She wore matching knit gloves and a lavender knit hat with a daisy at its crown. Sarah thought she looked adorable and fashionable as a former art teacher and painter should. Whiskey ran to romp with the poodles.

"Good morning, Sarah," Gladys called. "Brisk today."

"Hi, Gladys." Sarah gave her a hug. "It is a bit chilly, but at least the sun is shining."

"Always a glorious day when it's sunny. Did you get the registration for my girls? I found them the cutest outfits. I got Kahlo a beret and sweater. Both have a white background with red hearts. And for Cassatt I found a kissing booth head piece."

"Oh my. I can't wait to see them. Those sound perfect."

"Did you find Whiskey a costume yet?"

"He's not big on costumes. He doesn't like to wear coats or sweaters either. I think the best I can expect is for him to wear a red velvet bow tie on his collar."

"He's handsome as is, but that would make him debonair." Gladys reached a gloved hand to stroke Whiskey's head. He smiled up at her, like he understood what she said, his fluffy red and white-tipped tail swishing like a single windshield wiper, scattering the dusting of snow. Gladys continued, "I know, dear, you need to be on your way to make it to work on time. Thank you for stopping to say hello." And then to her poodles, she said, "Come on, girls, let's do your business so we can go back to the house and get warm."

Sarah kissed Gladys' cold cheek. "I'll come by this weekend for some tea and a chat."

"That would be lovely."

"I'll race you to the park entrance, Whiskey." Sarah jogged as she said the words, and Whiskey blew past her, his tongue hanging out, like "nah nah nah nah, You can't catch me."

Sarah chuckled and picked up speed, but she couldn't keep up with his four-legged gallop.

Whiskey sat and waited for her at the edge of Main Street, and then when Cottageville's only light turned green for their direction, they walked across the road and down a block to Java and Juice. Sarah opened the painted cherry door and the bell chimed overhead. Whiskey walked into the café ahead of her, his head held high, and went straight to the counter as no one was in line. One of his favorite humans and Sarah's boyfriend, Jared Greene, was behind the register. He gave Whiskey a homemade chicken biscuit after making him shake for it.

"Mi'lady." He acknowledged Sarah by bowing, in a silly schtick they had done since they first met years ago, but that had become more infrequent since they had become a couple in December.

"My lord." Sarah curtsied, holding out an imaginary skirt, and then handed him her tumbler, which he filled with black dark roast coffee, before passing it back to her. Sarah was surprised to see the café mostly empty. Two people Sarah didn't know, a middle aged man and an older woman, sat at one table near the bathroom. They looked deep in conversation.

Café owner Ginger Jones came from Java and Juice's back room, her arms ladened with trays of pastries. Her blond curls were pulled into a high ponytail, and she wore a charcoal thermal shirt beneath denim overalls, which were cuffed at the ankles above gray suede booties. "Hey, bestie," Ginger greeted Sarah. "I think you and Em need to try these." Ginger nodded her head toward the tray of scones that looked like they were liberally dotted with candy cinnamon hearts and dark chocolate chunks. "And I tried a new salad recipe today. Ginger beef with carrots, purple onions, greens, and udon noodles, so get that for lunch."

"What she said," Sarah said to Jared.

He took two scones from the tray Ginger set on the counter, before she bent to slide open the doors to the glass case so she could refill it. And then he turned to the cooler and picked up two salads and put those in the bag and then the scones on top. He threw in an extra biscuit for Whiskey for later, too. "May I make you supper tonight?" Jared asked as Sarah used her card to pay.

"I'd never say no to that." Sarah leaned across the counter and pressed her lips against his. "Come on, Whisk. We'll see Jared later. Bye, Ginger. I love you."

By the time Sarah arrived at Carter's Canine Coiffure, her assistant had already opened the business for the day and had Whiskey's pal seventy-five pounds of power Spike the pit bull, in the tub.

"Hey, Em," Sarah said, upon opening the green door of the Coiffure. She stopped short when she spied Daniel Snyder, owner of Buck and Son Hardware and Ginger's boyfriend, standing in the waiting room. The sight surprised Sarah, as Daniel and Ginger lived with no pets. "Hey, Daniel." Whiskey walked up to Daniel demanding some attention.

Daniel leaned down to scratch the dog's ears before standing upright again. "Sarah, I hope this is an okay time. I figured I'd catch you before you got too busy." He shifted his weight from his right foot to his left, but his eyes, golden brown the same color as Whiskey's, sought hers.

Sarah thought he looked more nervous than usual. "Let me put this bag down and take off my coat and I'll be right with you." Sarah put the salads in the fridge and the scones on the table in the back. She took off her winter wrappings and donned her denim dog print apron and then returned to the waiting area which was where the living room was when the building was someone's home.

Sarah remained standing since Daniel hadn't sat on the sofas. "So, what's up?" Sarah's green eyes bore into his.

"I need your help. Planning a surprise. For Ginger." His speech was more choppy than normal.

"Oh?" Sarah raised her eyebrows.

"I'm going... to ask her to marry me. But I need your help."

Sarah was squealing inside but trying to keep her cool. "Of course. Anything, Daniel. I'm so happy for both of you." She grabbed his forearm and squeezed. All of Cottageville knew the story as Daniel was a lifelong local: Daniel had married his high school sweetheart and had taken over the family's hardware store from his father while she worked as a paralegal at her father's law firm. They were overjoyed when they found out they were expecting a baby. Only, partway through the pregnancy, Daniel's wife hemorrhaged, and at the end of a workday, he found her collapsed in a puddle of blood on the kitchen floor. Both his unborn child and the love of his life were gone.

Years had gone by as he lived with the grief and went through the motions of life. But then last year, he asked Ginger, whom he had known since childhood, out on a date to a picnic next to a creek way outside of town. That one secretive date (so the whole town wouldn't know their business before they knew what they wanted) led to two and then to many, before Daniel sold the house he and his wife had lived in, and he and Ginger purchased an old farmhouse that they had been slowly remodeling, as they did much of the work themselves.

And though Ginger had confided in Sarah that she didn't care if they ever got married—especially if it would trigger trauma for Daniel—apparently, he felt differently. He was ready to pop the question and Sarah was sure Ginger would say yes. But what did he have in mind?

Sign up to follow Faith Walker and to never miss another Whiskey Dog Mystery release. Go to http://www.whiskeydogmysteries.com or follow us on social media @whiskeydogmysteries.